I dedicate this book to my husband Tom, and our four children, Peter, Kevin, Sheila and Thomas.

First published: November 2012
by Rena Gallogly
Copyright 2012

ISBN: 978-0-9574576-0-7

Designed by: Marla.ie
Printed by: Intacta Print Ltd.
Cover design: Marla.ie
Cover Photograph: Ian D Ryan

www.theshadowofthemountain.com

Foreword

For years I have enjoyed putting pen to paper, capturing unusual or funny incidents from everyday life. It wasn't until recently that I considered bringing all the stories together in book form. The result is *'The Shadow of the Mountain'*, a collection of short stories set primarily in rural Ireland, spanning the years from the mid 1990's to the present day. The stories will not only jog the memories of the older generation, but give younger people an insight into an Ireland they may never have known.

Acknowledgements

This book would not have been possible without the help and guidance of so many individuals. Some years ago, I joined the SARA Writers' Group, and take this opportunity to thank the members for their support.

Thanks to my many friends for their help and encouragement.

A special word of thanks to my husband, Tom, who kept me on the straight and narrow - I could always rely on him for a truly honest opinion!

To Lee Grace, at márla.ie whose expertise and skill transformed the book from script to text on screen. Thank you for your patience and great ideas.

And finally, to my daughter Sheila, who encouraged me to undertake this arduous task, and who brought the whole project together. I could not have done it without her!

Contents

Number Thirty-Five

Still no reply even though she had telephoned several times. She wanted this business to be dealt with as quickly as possible. She would try again in the late afternoon. In the meantime there was work to be done, starting with the garden. It had been totally neglected over the summer months. Today was ideal for the task. The sky was blue and a mischievous light wind sent the first of the autumn leaves chasing down the little path that led to the pond at the bottom of the garden.

'I must remember to cover it,' Nancy thought rather absentmindedly.

'Could save me a lot of trouble later.' She tended the flowers gently; they, too, were almost at the end of their time. In another few weeks she would plant all the winter bulbs, but she hadn't the heart to do it now. She worked solidly for several hours and was surprised to find how quickly time had passed when she stopped to look at her watch. It was the first time in months that she had been able to concentrate and enjoy what she was doing.

Finally the phone call came.

'We've been round to see the house. It's in very good condition for such an old one. By the way, there is a lot of stuff that will have to be cleared out before we put it up for sale. I'm sure there are things you want to take before the auction. Anything in particular you would like me to put aside?'

'No. Just clear it all. There's nothing of any value in it. The furniture can be auctioned too. None of it would suit here. The rooms are much smaller.' The voice at the other end of the phone showed no surprise.

'Whatever you say. Just as long as you're sure.'

She felt tired, the kind of fatigue that sleep does not relieve. Shortly after the ten o'clock news she fell into bed and finally dozed off. Nancy's dream was always the same. She was a little girl again, living in Number Thirty-Five, that big old rambling house, with her parents and her brother. Those were happy times, her mother busy at her knitting, her father reading his newspaper. The new baby was due shortly. She always woke at the point where her mum was packing her small bag '*en route*' for the hospital, proudly folding the little white matinee coat she had finished and placing it at the top of the case.

Still, she slept better than she had done for several weeks and it was the early morning noises that aroused her; the monotonous drone of car engines, punctuated only by the louder motion of an occasional tractor or the still louder noise of the big trucks as they passed her bedroom window. She was never aware of them during the day but they never failed to waken her in the early morning. She lay in bed for some time listening to the patter of rain on the window pane. Nothing she could do in the garden today. She thought again about her dream. On sudden impulse she jumped out of bed. Yes, there was something she could do. She would pay one last visit to Number Thirty-Five. Perhaps there were still some papers and letters there that should not be left lying around for strangers to read. She needed to check that drawers and presses had been cleared of their contents.

The heavy oak door creaked as she opened it. Once inside she put her shoulder to it out of habit, in order to close it. They had always had difficulty in getting it to close fully.

'Must do something about that door,' her father used to say, over and over again, but he never did. The sitting room with its big bay window was cosy and comfortable, warmed by little rays of sunshine that strove gallantly to dispel the morning gloom. The pink carpet and the floral suite looked warm and welcoming. Nancy had always loved this room and its familiarity seemed to soothe her now. She looked around at all the photographs, one of Joseph and herself holding the new baby. That had been such a happy day, the day of his Christening. He was named Brian after his grandfather. As she looked at the photo she felt a pang of guilt! She hadn't thought about Brian for a long time but then she had never had time to get to know him properly. He was just a little baby who had come into their lives for a short time and had left them far too quickly. She remembered too, that as a child, she had sometimes wished that he had never been part of them. The hurt, when he had died so suddenly that Hallowe'en night, had been too intense. Even now the scar was there. Her mother had never got over it. None of them had. For a while they had talked but, little by little, their silence reflected the deep pain that had taken root in each one of them.

Moving to the corner cabinet, she opened it and saw that it was still jammed with boxes, neatly piled on top of each other, some with photographs, others with cards and letters and slips of paper. One in particular caught her attention, the big Cadbury's Chocolate box tied with a large blue ribbon. Nancy remembered that she had, on a number of occasions, seen her mother push it quickly into the cabinet when she came into the room. Curiosity prompted her to have a quick look. The little baby wrist bands were there; all three, Baby Nancy Maguire, 7lb 2oz, Baby Joseph Maguire, 8lb 6oz and Baby Brian Maguire, 6lb 3oz. If he had lived he would have been in his twenties now. All the 'New Baby Boy' cards were there too, some from people she had long forgotten. One she recognised was from the cousins in Canada, who had been so kind to her younger brother when he had emigrated. The first time he had come home was for their father's funeral. It was just as if he had never left and they had chatted together into the small hours of the morning. He had stayed for almost three weeks and had been a great help to his mother and to herself. Last month, when he had come for their mother's funeral, they weren't as comfortable with each other as they had been in the past. Perhaps his recent divorce was responsible for his reticence. His visit had been short. Once the funeral was over he was in a hurry to get back 'home'. Before he had left on that miserably wet September morning, she had attempted one last time to get his attention.

'What about the house? Will we sell it?'

'You're the one who is living here so do what you think best. We can sort it out later.' That was over a month ago and he had only phoned once.

It was at the back of the tall press in the kitchen that she found another box with the tiny blue mittens her mother had bought for Brian the day they had gone shopping in Clery's. They were in cotton and put on his tiny hands at night so that he wouldn't scratch his face again with those little sharp nails. The doctor had said the infantile eczema would clear up as he got older. They had never had the chance to know! She rubbed the small mittens against her damp cheek and closed her eyes. She was sure she could get that lovely baby smell that was Brian's. Then she saw the little white matinee coat that her mother had knitted, the one that was always part of her dream, and suddenly she began to cry. She hadn't been able to do so since her mother had died. She sobbed her heart out and cried for her dad and Baby Brian and her mother and Joseph and herself, heaving great big sighs as though her heart was going to break. She examined the little feeding bottles packed so neatly in a row, the way her mother had always done. She had an obsession with tidiness, keeping both the house and garden in immaculate condition. Maybe that was part of the problem when cancer had robbed her of her freedom and independence. She had never been one to give in to aches and pains and it had progressed extensively by the time she sought help. She no longer had the energy to do the things she wanted and her world was suddenly turned upside down. Then the trips to Dublin had begun, each visit to the hospital a greater nightmare than the previous one, as chemotherapy took its toll. Nancy was finding it almost impossible to cope. She no longer recognised her mother in this skeleton of a woman, who became more and more demanding. She had moved back into Number Thirty-Five to be with her. There were nights when she fell into bed completely exhausted, only to waken to the tinkle of the little bell from her mother's room, as she strove to find some relief from the excruciating pain that racked her body. The doctors told her the cancer had attacked her spine, and, though drugs and painkillers brought some relief, she suffered to her death. The time came when she had to move into the hospice. Nancy drove to the city every day and dreaded the moment when she would see her mother's emaciated face as she entered the room. That had lasted for three months. She was relieved when her heart had given up. When it all ended she had no tears left to shed. Exhaustion had taken over and she no longer knew who she was and no longer cared.

The afternoon had brightened up after the morning's rain. Only when the light had faded to semi-darkness did she become aware that she had spent hours in the house, piecing together the life of the Maguire family. Each room had its own story and suddenly it became important to her. It was all that remained to her now. What about Joseph? She owed it to both of them to sort things out. She would phone him that very night and try to find out what had been on his mind when he had come for the funeral. She knew that she had complained incessantly about how tired she was feeling and how difficult her mother's illness had been for her. She realised now that she had not given him a chance to talk. His divorce must have been difficult for him and perhaps he felt guilty that he hadn't come home more often. It was her turn to listen! They could have good times together again.

The phone call to the auctioneer's was short and to the point.

'I've decided not to sell Number Thirty- Five after all. I'll be moving there myself. My own bungalow will be for sale but that won't be for some time yet. There's a lot of work to be done on the old house.' The secretary paused for a moment before replying.

'I'll pass the message on to Mr Kelly when he comes in. Ms Maguire, I'd just like to wish you the very best of luck. It's such a beautiful house.' Anne felt a surge of happiness and excitement as ideas began to take hold. That old wallpaper in the hall would have to be changed for a start and perhaps the wall between the dining room and the sitting room could be knocked to let in more light. She would get proper plans drawn up and... her mind began to race as she thought of all the things she could do to make the house a home once more.

Her face was brighter and her step lighter as she left, pulling the old heavy oak door behind her.

'I'll have to do something about that door,' she said to herself with a smile.

Spring

Another spring has come round. I am up in time to see the hoar frost still shrouding the front window. It came stealthily overnight and is quite heavy. Long before midday the pane of glass will be clear again to give full view of the rose bushes, which have been pruned in anticipation of the new season. Yesterday I saw the first of the new baby buds on the bare branches of the chestnut trees. The snowdrops have raised their heads and are already comfortably established. They are graceful and elegant, curtsying, all in white, like a *'debutante'* taking pride of place at a first ball.

I enjoy the luxury of a long, leisurely breakfast. Spring is definitely in the air. My spirits are high. Winter has lost its grip. I am free again; free from the overcast skies, which have weighed heavily upon me; above all, free from the wintry fears and turbulences within.

I set about the early morning chores on automatic overdrive. My step is light. There is a brightness in the sky that I haven't seen for months and which is reflected within me. A transparent ray of sunshine falls on the kitchen cupboard, revealing the finger marks on the knobs. There will be many a rainy day to take care of such trivialities! I can clearly detect my little grandson's grubby finger marks on the patio door. I'm loathe to do anything about them (even when that rainy day comes). I feel a lightness in my heart when I look at them. As long as they are there I can feel the presence of that lovely little baby boy. They are probably there since his last visit at Christmas when he took his first hesitant steps towards the door and laughed with delight at his success. He won't ever remember but I will. I've never noticed them before but spring's slanting sunshine has brought them to light.

I go outside to get something from the car. The lock on the door is frozen. I enjoy pouring the hot kettle over it before attacking the windows, front and rear. I am like a child playing a game. Traffic along the road is the same as always, folks rushing on their way to somewhere. In the thin, sunny, frosty air the noise is lighter, more restrained. A delivery truck trundles past, its number plate barely visible through the residue of dust and dirt, built up over the wet, stormy months of winter. Now that spring has come its driver may give it a much-needed wash. A bunch of children on their way to the school bus pass along the wall beside me. I greet them but only one of them acknowledges me. The others are so busy chatting that they are not aware of my presence. Two of the smaller ones fall into a skipping pattern and as they move away I can hear them sing 'Here We Go Gathering Nuts in May'. It is years since I heard that rhyme. May too, will come. I look forward to it.

Two robins sing to each other and to me. They, too, are glad that spring has arrived. Soon they will build their nests. Are they mates or just courting? I am a part of all that is taking place, sharing in the wonderful joy of yet another spring unfolding all around me. I feel the presence of someone or something. The loneliness and isolation of a winter world are behind me now.

The Bell

It was a small town where the same things happened at the same time every day. First came the sound of the early Mass Bell. Not everyone headed for the church but we all heard the bell. I loved its rich tone and took to counting its tolls - one, two, three, four. It rang twelve times in all. We wondered about the sacristan whose job it was to send the peals across the air. He was always dressed in black. I figured that he was only half a priest and was always a little in awe of him. He never spoke to us and somehow looked old. He walked with a bit of a crouch but I felt that carrying the big Mass Book, the huge candelabra and ringing the bell had stunted his growth and left him with a hump. Maybe when he'd learn to walk straight he'd be fully qualified to become a real priest! The one we had was a cross old man, who terrified us when he came into the school and asked us silly questions. The bell ringer had a lovely kind face and I'm sure his voice would have been gentle too.

It was the noisy chatter of the first group of men, returning from the eight o'clock Mass, that signalled to our neighbour, Annie Owens, that it was time to open her front door from where she viewed the familiar morning scene.

'Morning Mary,' was always lost on her; she was more interested in the women who were quietly chatting at Rose Rooney's door. She never went up to join them; she thought they were a gossipy lot, a crowd of newsbags. They'd be better off not going to Mass at all if they were spreading lies about people. She never gave them the benefit of the doubt; after all they might only be discussing the price of basic necessities and asking after their families. When they'd finally scatter she'd move closer to the footpath with her sweeping brush, cleaning the pavement, which was never dirty anyway. She swept until the postman came into sight. It was nice to see who got a letter and who didn't. That young Smith fellow hadn't written to his mother for months now. She'd miss the few pounds he'd regularly sent her. Maybe he had lost his job but, although she knew his mother well, she would never stoop to ask for news. She had her own way of finding out what she needed to know. Minnie Watters was a mine of information and she often dropped in mid-morning for a cup of tea. She loved the 'cuppa' and in between the sips of tea and the four Marietta biscuits (which she invariably swallowed in halves) she brought Mary up to date on the latest. She was never in a hurry to go but as soon as the Angelus Bell rang at twelve o'clock she'd get up from her chair, pat the cushion and take her leave, always with the same farewell.

'I'll be off now. Better get home to put the knife and fork down on the table before himself comes in for a bite of dinner.'

By now it's business of the day for all. The small grocery shop is busy, four or five customers all at once. The butcher has sold all the lamb shanks and is running out of diced beef. It's weather for stew and the children will soon be out of school, running down the hill for something to eat. A few hardy characters cross themselves with an apologetic hand as the Bell continues to ring and the women in the butcher's pray the Angelus. Only the noise of the cleaver breaks the silence as he rushes to cut the fatty bits of lamb for Mrs White, availing of the blessed moment to pull the wool over her eyes. Only on one occasion had she protested with

'Hold it there, Michael. I'm praying that God will give you

pardon for your sins.' Then she whispered to Hannah Gallagher

'Keep a good eye on him when he's givin ye a shin bone with the meat. He'd charge ye for the weight o' the bone if ye didn't watch him. He has fooled the smartest of them; he fooled meself.'

None of the conversation is lost on Michael, who quickly hides the lumpy, fatty bits of meat under the greaseproof paper. He throws one big piece of fat into the sawdust on the floor, anxious to keep his customer happy in the belief that she had, for once, pulled him into line.

For my part, I fondly cherish many happy memories of the Bell. I remember its sound as Mary, my friend and I, twiddled our toes in a clear crystal stream, watching the water trickle over our feet. It was the Easter holidays and we were making big plans for the next summer ones, trying to decide what kind of sandwiches we would make for all the picnics. Just then the Angelus rang. It was warm for April, the sun was shining and as we stopped to pray we were a happy pair.

'Behold the handmaid of the Lord.'

'Do you want mustard on your ham ones?'

'No.'

'Be it done unto me according to Thy word.'

'Don't forget I hate brown sauce.'

'Holy Mary…'

'But I love egg ones without onion.' On it went! I don't remember whether we ever had those picnics beside the stream that summer, but the enthusiasm we shared for the grand culinary delights to be eaten ' *al fresco*' still sets my taste buds in action. We needed no picnic that day; the imaginary one was far better.

In short, the Church Bell punctuated our days. When it rang on the first Saturday of the month at twelve o' clock we hurried to the church for the children's confessions at twelve thirty. It was a lengthy process. The priest wandered in after us when our examination of conscience had long been completed and the Confiteor said. On one occasion he was very late and very bothered. We figured that his housekeeper, who ruled the roost, had fallen out with him. Anyway, he was extremely angry because we had all begun to talk and laugh. He threatened not to hear our confessions. I'd have been delighted but he passed on that one! That week at least, I knew I had to add one extra sin to my usual ones; talking in the chapel. I was rather pleased with myself, as I had become tired of reciting the same list month after month. I stuck it in halfway through.

'I was bold.

I told lies.

I talked in the chapel.

I didn't do what my mother told me.

I didn't say my prayers on Monday night because I fell asleep.'

I got it all off my chest in record time and would soon be on my way home. I wasn't afraid of the priest now that we were both in the box. Our teacher had told us that even if you killed a man, you were telling that sin to God. He would forgive you; the priest was only taking the place of God. When I heard a voice bellowing at me through the little dark, mesh window I nearly had a fit. This wasn't what I had expected! I got the fright of my life. I don't know where God was that day but He was not in the confessional. I'd have to be more careful in future.

In a strange way, the evening Angelus Bell marked the end

of the day. Shopkeepers began to tidy up for the closure of their premises at 7.00pm (or 7.30, if a possible customer was spotted viewing the wares in the window). Children were sent to the shop to get a loaf of bread for the evening tea and the next morning's breakfast. My sister and I were always under orders to return home from playing on the street when the evening bell rang. For years I looked forward to the day when I would be old enough to be allowed out after tea. When it did come I found it all most disappointing. As with so many other things in childhood, anticipation was more fulfilling than participation.

Then there were the funerals when the church bell rang out again, its sombre peals somehow different from the everyday Angelus Bell. I still loved its rich, mellow tones, which conveyed nothing of the sadness of death to us youngsters. When a neighbour, aged forty, died suddenly, I was amazed to hear my father say

'He was so young.'

Forty! Who would want to live that long? Death meant nothing to us. I cried when my grandfather died because I knew I would never see him again. We weren't allowed to go to the funeral. We were sheltered from the sadness and shock of seeing a coffin go into the ground. That would come later.

So it was that the Angelus Bell and all church bells were a part of my life. I loved them and bonded with them wherever I went. Away from home, in boarding school, the cathedral clock striking ten was the signal for 'Lights Out' in the dormitory where I slept, bringing a sort of comfortable loneliness for home. I felt close to my parents.

Today, being of mature years, the Angelus Bell on RTE,

just before the evening news, is a precious moment of calm and reflection in my day. While the debate continues as to whether or not the peals of an Angelus Bell should be broadcast on our country's main TV channel I enjoy it for what it conveys to me.

The Enemy

I opened the hot press door and recoiled in fear and dismay. Another one and nobody here to remove the evidence but me. It was smaller than my thumb and yet my whole body tightened with tension and my heart was pounding while a death march drummed in my ears. I stared at the bunched-up little corpse on its final wooden resting place and I was suddenly overwhelmed with remorse.

Why did I hate them so? It's over thirty years since my first encounter with mice. That autumn we had moved to our new home, unaware that workmen had left scraps of food under floorboards and in various locations throughout the house. The carpentry work had not yet been fully completed. The family, or families of mice, had squatted and were nicely settled in before we, the new occupants, arrived. It was only when we realised that we were sharing the same toaster that we became aware of their presence.

Since then I have often wondered if I'm the only person to have witnessed a mouse having a heart attack. Once we realised we had a problem we placed traps under the sink, where the plumber had cut a generous opening around the water pipes, a haven for the mice. On one particular morning, my husband had disposed of a number of them and declared,

'That was a good night's catch.' He reset the traps before leaving for work. I felt quite happy and pleased with the result. No more intruders! There could not be any left so I opened the cupboard door just as a trap snapped. Another victim lay inert, after a brief struggle. It was then that I saw another poor little mite in a sitting position on the new white Formica shelf. Mice can hardly turn pale but I'm sure this one did! Those beady little eyes seemed to say,

'How could you?' Then, to my dismay, the little body shook and shivered and quivered and the mouse suffered a heart attack, twirled around and collapsed on the spot. It was a little beauty, with an exquisite, miniature body and long round ears. I stood in shock and then felt hot tears on my cheeks. I was crying as I looked at the corpse lying on its side. To this day I feel guilty about that one little baby that had died from fright. Was it the snap of the trap or the sight of me that had caused the heart attack? Was I guilty of murder or manslaughter? I will never know.

The Fair Day

I should have known better! I tried to open our front door and ended up on my rear end with six lambs rushing into the hallway. Hearing the commotion my father came running.

'Don't you know we don't use this door on Fair Days?' Taking hold of the sweeping brush he turned the poor things onto the street again. How could I have forgotten! Hadn't I heard the noise of the animals and their owners in my sleep from the early hours of the morning, as they took their places along the street and settled in for the long wait. It was now nine o'clock and the serious business of the day, the buying and selling of stock, was in full swing. At least ten sheep were tied to the knocker and handle of our front door. They would stay there until sold. There was nothing unusual about that. It was the one day in the month when the town was taken over by the local farmers and cattle dealers, wheelers and dealers with the usual sprinkling of chancers. It was, literally, the day the cow calved for the town and there was a bit of money to be made.

We children loved the Fair Day and were a part of it all. School was closed which was a real bonus. Nobody minded a bunch of youngsters hanging around and we did have our uses. Sometimes we were called on to buy a couple of Woodbines in the corner shop or asked to keep an eye on the animals while the owner went off for a wee drop of porter. The reward was generous, a couple of pennies for a few sweets or a 'Peggy's Leg'. Life was free and easy and our parents knew we were safe. They never told us not to talk to strangers; we were all friends who met once a month. We came to know the regulars and would head for the spot where the drama was likely to be at its best. For a short period in my childhood I thought that a 'fecker' was the brother of a heifer!

'Ye don't expect me to give ye the colour o' what ye're askin' for those little feckers!' We waited for the look of hurt on the face of the seller at this outrageous insult as the prospective buyer turned on his heel, only to be coaxed back by a third party. We'd move closer as the bargaining progressed, over and back and back again. Time was on hold, we waited in suspense as the best was yet to come. We held our breath for the final curtain, which came with a long spit, never missed, on the palm of the hand. It was followed by a mighty handshake and a hearty slap on the back. We longed for the day when we would be able to reach such heights of skill with some degree of accuracy. Sometimes the tired animals at the centre of these negotiations, oblivious of all the proceedings, relieved themselves in the middle of the crowd and we'd make a hasty retreat until the pungent smell died down. I still remember the smells of Fair Days, which varied according to the season. In winter, everything was heavy with the scent of damp and turf smoke, while in summer, there was a warm sweet odour like the smell of hay. In the forties 'hygiene' was just a word in the dictionary, confined to the bookshelves of those who did not dare venture out on Fair Days.

The Bank was an establishment of great importance and had a very important role to play. Not so much as a financial institution but as a windbreaker for the farmer and his animals, because it formed a kind of L-Shape with the pub next door and that space was much in demand. It was a simple matter of getting your tail in first and letting the best man win. The one who succeeded was set up for the day and could have the odd bottle of stout while still in full view of his charges. There was the occasional mini-crisis, nothing too serious. One smart man decided to tie his sheep across the entrance to the Bank garage, an ideal spot! When the Manager finally located the culprit in one of the many pubs in town he was most indignant and announced that he had a very important meeting in Dublin next morning.

'Sure what hurry is on ye? Can't ye go tomorrow or the next day? They'll know you're comin one of these days. Sure ye'll be as right as rain!'

In the afternoon it was the women's turn to enjoy what remained of the day. The stalls, or 'standings', filled most of the Upper Main Street and sold everything from porringers (or 'pongers') to second-hand clothes. Business was brisk and many's the youngster was rigged out for the important occasion at bargain prices. Supply didn't always meet demand but the buyer never went away empty-handed.

'If it was any smaller it'd look a holy show on him ma'am. The weather can often be fierce cold in June.' Five minutes later another aspiring Confirmation candidate was measured up for his outfit.

'He's a growing boy and ye'll find it'll nearly be too small for him in six weeks time.' The unfortunate victim, rarely consulted, was known to have gone off with a suit three times his size. When Joe Rooney brought his son for a fitting the lad took flight and ran down the street. He disappeared into a doorway and could not be found. Joe asked everybody he met if they had seen him.

'I can't find me son. Did ye see a gossoon about thon high, a good looking boy, running away? I'm afraid I lost him. He's a nervous young lad like his mother and to tell ye the truth I'm nervous meself.' Joe Junior was finally spotted in a snug, drinking red lemonade and the jacket was never mentioned again.

The Fair leading up to Christmas was very special when there were stalls of all descriptions and sizes in every nook and cranny of the town. "The Bargain King's" stall was one of the most sought after.

'One tomato will feed all your lodgers if you buy this knife,' and he proceeded to give a demonstration with a ripe red tomato, the offending knife and a running commentary that brought peals of laughter from the crowd. He sold every one of the knives. I remember one particular day when Confessions in the local Church clashed with the beat on the street. My mother and her friend had both gone, each to a different priest, in order to hurry things up. Unfortunately Father John was very slow and the queue hardly moved. My mother, waiting outside became very impatient, and finally asked me to see if there was any sign of Mary. I headed into the Church and there she was, up at the Altar rails, in the process of making her Confession. Both she and the priest had their heads bowed in anonymity.

'Excuse me, Father, but my Mammy says if you don't let Mary out soon all the good delph will be gone and there'll be nothing but a load of rubbish left.' Funny thing was that nobody but the priest seemed to appreciate my efforts.

Next to the pubs the favourite haunts on Fair Days were the many establishments that fed the hungry. The more traditional souls referred to these as 'Eatin Houses'. Business was brisk and the choice limited. Most popular was the meat tea or the dinner, usually with a request not to spare the meat! Everyone knew where to go for a good feed. One house carried a simple advert in the window, which read 'Tay Wet'. Gallons of tea were poured on those days and all were satisfied, although the day never ended without a row. Fists were used to score some point or other. There was always a crowd to support one side or the other. It never lasted too long and the pair usually ended up shaking hands and even going as far as the pub for that last pint. It was all in good spirits and egged on by a rogue among them who wanted to end the day having his bit of fun.

'I "rise" that,' he'd whisper to his friends as the two able-bodied men fought furiously. Bets were taken with a shout.

'Let the best man win!'

As evening fell the town emptied, except for a few lost souls.

'Did you not go home yet?'

'No. Did you?'

It was late when the last stragglers headed away, except for the lone drunk, loathe to leave, invariably ending the day with a raucous rendering of 'I'll Take You Home Again Kathleen'. Then it was time to start on the big clean up. Unfortunately, the man who had been doing it for donkey's years had never come to grips with the workings of the hose. The result was that most of the dung ended up on the walls of the houses. For several days there was washing up and washing down and up and down again until gradually the place took on a semblance of normality. Then we all settled down to get ready for the next Fair Day.

The Parting

It's his first day at school and I know in my heart of hearts that he doesn't really believe all I've told him. Yet I love him so much that it's easier to let him find out for himself that the world is not as sunny as I had led him to believe. Now the time has come to say 'goodbye' but the words won't come. I look at him and at that moment he looks at me. We two are alone, alone among a group of noisy children, four of them mine, awaiting the arrival of the bus. The little face with those keen, sharp eyes searches for a sign, assuring him that it's going to be all right. I smile at him and what do I feel? A hint of betrayal? Have I denied him? The conflict within me is disturbing. I have deceived him, and for the first time I'm really letting him down. Worse still, I realise that I'm no longer fully in control.

Yes, he's growing up and away from me. Glimpses of other partings inevitably to follow pass before me. Short holidays with a few tears, railway station goodbyes, with a cautious kiss, then, airports, with only a casual wave or maybe none. And one day a girlfriend, to become his wife? Again, my feelings disturb me. Do I feel jealous already that one day his love must surely be given to another?

He grasps my hand tighter. The bus has come. Suddenly he knows he doesn't want to go. I don't want him to go either, but I mustn't let him know. Again this sense of hypocrisy almost stifles me. Is it a pattern of life? The little deceptions, unimportant at first, until they interfere with the rightful decisions of another. Those simple half-truths, which we insinuate aren't really lies, just conveniences. And where do we leave honesty?

He's up the first step of the bus when he turns and cries,

'Mammy, I don't want to go.' I don't know from where I muster the courage to say sharply,

'You're going. No nonsense.' He knows I mean business and he takes his place, tears on his cheeks, beside his older brother.

And so the blow has been dealt to him and to me. We've parted. He's on the bus and off to school. I never felt such emotion when the others first went. But then he's the last. It's a new chapter for him but the closing of one for me. Something of an awful sadness grips me. I pull myself together as my neighbour beams,

'Has he gone?' I manage a smile and a 'Yes,' but she knows and I know that it would be easier to be honest and cry. I'll save that for later!

Back in the kitchen the tears come freely. It's just the way I cried the day he was born – relief, joy, sadness, all in one. A mother's pain! The coffee remains hot to the end this morning; no calls for help from the bathroom, and suddenly, I'm at it again – how will he manage on his own? But I'm only a spectator now, no longer his manager. I settle down to the daily household chores but my heart is heavy.

The door opens and he runs to me, the same small little boy. But things have changed and will never be the same. He has taken the jump and I'm glad it's over. It's consoling to hear him say

'Mammy, won't you wave to me every morning until you get so small that I cannot see you.' Thank God, he still has faith in me!

Bridging the Gap

Kate was only nine but very tall for her age. She loved being as big as her older sister. Everyone thought they were twins, which they weren't, but it was great fun anyway. They had collected quite a lot of money over the years, under false pretences, but by the time the donors found out it was too late. They could hardly ask for their money back!

'Such lovely little girls! What age are you? Here, get yourselves some sweets.' They never gave an answer until the money was safely in their hands!

She's glad to be going back to school again. Mum had kept her at home because of that chesty cough. What she could never understand was why her mother got so cross with her when she caught cold. It wasn't her fault. Well, maybe sometimes it was, like that last rainy day when she had dallied all the way home, walking through every puddle she could find until her feet were soaking. She just loved it and wanted to get as wet as she possibly could. But her Mum got really mad with her, especially when she coughed and coughed.

Now she was almost ready. Her mother had put the lovely red ribbons in her hair and stood back to look her over. Just then she began to cough and for one awful moment she was afraid she wouldn't let her go.

'You look so pale,' she said. Kate did not answer. She just held her breath to make sure she wouldn't cough again. She wasn't bothered about looking pale; the cold sores were what bothered her and she wished her nose would stop dripping. She looked again at her feet. She hated the long stockings that Mum had made her wear. It was only September and she would get all kinds of funny looks at break-time but there was nothing she could do about that. Anyway, they wouldn't dare say a word to her because Brenda would give a bloody nose to anyone who insulted her younger sister. Still, she hated being different and wished she didn't have to stay away from school so often.

Maybe the teacher wouldn't pick on her about her sums anymore. She was always behind the others and hated being told she wasn't paying attention. Sums bored her and no matter how hard she tried she always started to daydream instead of following what Ms Clarke was pointing out on the blackboard.

Today was no different. Lost in the complications of water going in and out of a bath at the same time and with words like volume and speed and gallons coming at her from a distance the teacher's voice began to drift away and Kate with it. She was in a different world where she could make everything right. She wanted to be a teacher, or maybe a doctor, and be kind to everybody. For now, she had chosen to be a teacher and she was standing in front of a class of smiling children. She knew she was daydreaming but wanted to believe it.

'Yes dear, I'll explain it to you. It's so easy!' and all the little darlings, including her daughter in the front row, understood it all. School would finish in half an hour and her handsome husband would be waiting at the gate in his car to whisk them both…

Everyone was staring at her and Mary Brown was giggling nervously beside her.

'You're not listening again. So, what's new! Repeat what I've just said, madam!' and Teacher was staring and staring at her, ready to pounce. She hated it when the teacher called her 'madam' and she hadn't a clue what she was going to say.

'Eh, the water going into the bath…and out' she said hoping for a reprieve but none came.

'What about it?'

'Well, I think it's going in faster than it's getting out.'

'Do you now!' You could hear a pin drop and Kate's cheeks were burning.

'I'm not sure, Miss, of the right answer.'

'Of course you're not. Now Mary Brown, you've been listening. You tell us all about it.'

She'd just have to pretend that she was interested and she propped her two hands under her chin and tried her best to concentrate. With a bit of luck she might even get the next answer right. What she would really like to say was that it was awfully wasteful to be letting water in and out of the bath at the same time. It was all so complicated and no fun at all. Anyway, she was right about the water going in faster than it got out because their bath was always getting blocked up with hairs and fluffy stuff and she just loved to watch her Dad get at it with an old clothes hanger. He always managed to sort it out. Then they'd both laugh at the way the water suddenly chugged and gurgled down the drain. This other business of volume and speed was all too serious. Teacher was missing out on the real fun in life! She would love to tell her that, but she knew she couldn't…

………………..

And so the years passed by, slowly at first, with its rhythm of seasons, each bringing its old familiarities and its changes too. Some of these changes were so subtle that they went almost unnoticed, like the ticking of the clock on the mantelpiece. It is only when the clock strikes that one sits up and takes notice. When Kate was twelve her mother died. She and Brenda had to grow up quickly. Their father was not a great man to talk. When he did speak of their mother it was in a roundabout way that did not invite questions from his daughters.

'Mammy would (or would not) be very pleased with you about such and such.' They both knew he was hurting and tried to avoid any conversation that might upset him. He seemed to think that if he kept his grief safely locked up within him it would somehow lessen his feeling of loss. He never thought about all the questions the two girls wanted to ask. Why did their mother have to die and why did nobody talk to them about it? It was all whispers and hush-hush when they were around. Her death made no sense to them. Just when they needed her most she was gone.

Years later, when Kate and Brenda had married and had families of their own, Aunt Catherine, home on a visit from the States, brought an old photo album with her. As Kate and she browsed over the snapshots the resemblance between her own daughter, Eileen, and the picture of her mother as a child, brought tears to her eyes. Catherine was a great woman to talk and used to drive their father mad with her 'prating', as he called it! It had been over five years since her last visit and she was certainly making up for lost time. She told Kate stories of her childhood days. As they chatted about the photos and the past Kate finally began to confide in her aunt.

'After Mum died I could not remember her face except in my dreams. I used to cry myself to sleep at night and when I tried to think about the good times we all had together I could only remember how she used to get cross with me. I seemed to have the knack of upsetting her. I still feel guilty about the things I did. I was so childish; like the day I climbed up on a chair to peep into the tall press in the kitchen to see if my birthday present was hidden there. I knocked down a bottle of perfume, which spilled all over the floor. It had been a present from Dad to Mum and now it was broken. I felt so awful and was sent to my bedroom until I was called down for tea. Mum had made lovely pancakes but I could hardly swallow them. I was so miserable.'

Suddenly Kate could not hold in the tears. Her sobs became louder and as she tried to control them, her daughter, Eileen, put her arms around her.

'Don't cry Mummy. What's wrong?' Aunt Catherine had settled herself in the big armchair and gently asked,

'What's all this about? Surely your Dad must have talked to you about your mother's illness all those years ago when you were very small. She used to fuss over you because you were the delicate one and she wanted to protect you. Did you not know that she was diagnosed with TB when you were only three? Don't you remember anything at all? You were still sleeping in a cot in your parents' room the first time she became ill. I was there at the time.'

Something like a far-off dream began to surface in Kate's memory and she could hear her mother coughing near her. It was all hazy but very real. She was so small that she had to stand up in her cot to see what was going on. Yes! The old doctor was there. She liked him because he always had sweets in his pocket. He even had one for her then but it was hard and she found it difficult to chew. It was all so strange. Her dad was standing beside the bed and the old nurse, her mother's friend, was there too. She watched it all but could not understand any of it. Why was her mother crying? Something was not right. She rubbed her eyes to see if they were still there and she heard her mother coughing again. It was then that she heard the doctor say,

'Kate will have to be moved out of the room straight away. I'll make arrangements to get you a bed in hospital as soon as possible and try not to worry.' She didn't know what was happening but she knew she didn't like it. How could she not have remembered any of this before? Was that when her mother had gone away for what seemed a very long time? Aunt Catherine was talking on and on. Perhaps she hadn't remembered at all; maybe it was her aunt who was filling in the gaps for her. She had been very young then and it was such a long time ago. Maybe this had something to do with those dreams after her mother died. She had gone away; nobody could tell her where, so she waited and waited and her mother always came back. Each time she awoke she really believed mum had come back and for a few glorious minutes she was happy. Then reality hit. She was not coming back.

Now after all the years, it was her aunt who had opened up the past for her. A lot of things made sense - her mother's concern for her, the long absences from home. She felt a great sense of relief, but frustration and anger too. Why had their father not faced up to reality and shared his loneliness and pain with them? It would have been good for him and for them but it hadn't happened. He had decided what was best but how could he know? They desperately needed him to talk to them and he had let them down. Why could they not have shared the many happy memories of their mother to help them close the awful gap? Grief had had its term and they needed to move on…. together. That he had failed to do.

Maybe she was too hard on him. He was convinced he was doing the right thing and she knew he loved them both even if he never said so. Perhaps it wasn't his fault. Many others would have done the same thing, unable or perhaps unwilling, to talk about what was hurting them most. The false silence created had only caused that hurt to fester and grow.

She knew that in the past TB had been a killer, dreaded by all. A certain stigma and shame were often borne by those who had caught the disease. Another reason for his silence perhaps! Thankfully, with the introduction of antibiotics all that had changed, but even then, he had never broken his silence and their mother's death was not discussed.

Kate, now deep in thought, suddenly felt a great sense of relief surge through her whole being. She was finally coming to terms with the past. As she looked at her young daughter she became aware that a new understanding of herself, of life and of those whom she loved had kindled within her. She even felt compassion for her father who had shut himself away and suffered alone. She vowed that she would never fall into the trap.

Suddenly the sound of Aunt Catherine's voice aroused her.

'It's time I got out of here. I've promised Brenda to call to her tomorrow. She and I will have a long chat too and afterwards we are going to that lovely little café where they make those divine éclairs. I'd better say goodbye to that handsome husband of yours.' Still talking, Catherine took her farewell of the three of them. As her car moved out of the driveway Kate went into the living room where Philip was reading his newspaper, shoes off and feet stretched towards the warmth and comfort of the turf fire. She sat down beside him, took his hand and caressed it gently.

'What brought this on? Has Catherine been prating again?'

'I was just thinking that even people who love each other sometimes don't make time to talk.' Just as he was about to kiss her Eileen burst into the room.

'Mum, could I have some hot chocolate before I go to bed?'

'Let's all have hot chocolate and we'll melt marshmallows by the fire,' she answered. As Eileen raced into the kitchen Philip kissed Kate and with his mischievous smile whispered

'You should keep on thinking like that. I like it!'

The Walk

As she walked along the seashore the waves lapped gently at her feet. It was as though they sensed the feeling of terrible sadness and despondency that had enveloped her from early morning. The loud roar of the ocean from behind the sand dunes followed her as she paced along. At last she was alone with nature. She had walked this beach from the time she was a child, always at home here but now no longer at ease. She scarcely felt her body move; yet some force propelled her along.

Her thoughts were troubled and her whole being weighed heavily upon her. She felt trapped and wanted to escape, to break out. Was this really she or had some stranger taken over her body? What was happening? It had all been too much to absorb. She tried to make sense of it but how could she! Why had it come to this? In her heart she knew there was no point in questioning. There were no answers. Nothing was going to change.

She raised her eyes and watched the mist coming down on the hill. It was so beautiful that it took her by surprise and she stopped in her tracks for a few moments as it covered the sheer end of the hill nearest to her. Bit by bit it dropped and as it did so, the familiar face of the rise became veiled, as another scene unfolded. The familiar had become unfamiliar but its beauty could not be surpassed. She rounded the grassy mound where she usually ended her walk but today she decided to continue on. For now, time was on her side and she needed to come to terms with the confusion within.

She needed to concentrate on what was happening to her. Still in shock, she felt as though she were dreaming. Perhaps she would waken up at any moment to the monotonous familiar daily routine, a welcome relief from this nightmare of reality. As she walked the sand became so soft that she had difficulty in keeping her step. Her breathing quickened with the effort and again she paused to rest, as she viewed the scene before her.

The tide had begun to ebb, but little ripples of water circled around her toes. Their coolness comforted her and she no longer felt the chill of the sharp wind that had accompanied her all along the headland. In this little cove it was like a summer's day. The sun came through the clouds for a few moments and she felt a warmth and sense of feeling come into her tired body. Tears flowed freely, as she acknowledged this moment of respite. She stood quietly, calmly, all alone in the silence of her thoughts. She needed to hold on to this, needed to remember it for what lay ahead, an unknown dimension, which terrified her. She must never forget what she was witnessing. Never! How long was 'Never'? Nothing was fixed or constant anymore.

For now she was suspended in time, as in a still life painting. If only the moment could go on forever. Did she imagine it, or had the sea calmed even more, little ripples seeming to hold their movement? Just for her? She closed her eyes and the picture held fast. This would help to sustain her for what lay ahead. It was all so beautiful; sea, sky, sand, green hills sloping gently downwards. She had seen it all before but never like this. Perhaps there was a message in it for her. That she could not say.

Suddenly, a huge wave came crashing on the boulders to her right. A few sea gulls, taken by surprise, screeched raucously as they flew overhead. She felt cheated and tears stung her eyes. It was cruel. The precious moment had been snatched from her. It was gone, gone forever.

She continued her walk but now the sense of hopelessness was swelling up within her once again and with it a feeling of anger. All around, the familiar sounds, which, a few moments ago, had been such a comfort to her, no longer supported her and almost seemed to mock. She felt so alone, so isolated. What scared her most was the realization that she had to go through this all on her own. She could finish it now by walking out into the ocean. That would be so easy, too easy, the coward's way out. But was it? What was she facing? From where would she find the strength and courage in the terrible weeks and months that lay ahead? There was no escape.

Suddenly she turned and began to walk briskly back. Now the cold air stung her as she rounded the corner. A young couple, hand in hand, greeted her as she climbed the slope. She returned their greeting with a smile.

'Isn't she very pretty?' the young girl remarked.

'Yes, I suppose so! She doesn't seem to have a care in the world,' her friend replied, as the woman disappeared behind the sand dunes.

The Station Mass

I couldn't believe my luck! My mother had agreed that I could go to the country for a few days, all on my own. As I skipped down the footpath to pick up the weekly groceries I could scarcely conceal my delight.

'Mammy says to put it in the book. She'll pay you for all next week'. Every week I was sent to the grocer's with the same message. She did pay eventually but there was always one week owing.

I was to travel by bus, a real treat, to my mother's cousins, who lived just five miles away. I nodded in agreement to all the orders I was given...bed in time, help with the chores, I must not annoy Cissie, the older sister, with my constant chattering. On and on! For once I was afraid to speak in case she would change her mind but then the bus came round the corner.

'She'll be getting off at the far crossroads and her dad will collect her on his bicycle on Friday.' Neither my mother nor the bus conductor addressed any of the conversation to me.

'I won't charge her, Ma'am. Sure she's only a little nipper.' I was quite grown-up, all of eight-years-old and I didn't like being called a 'nipper' but I held my peace. I felt six feet tall as I sat in the front seat waving to my mother as she stood on the pavement. I was on my way at last to the far crossroads. A light frost still lay on the fields, clothing them in white gossamer. Later in the day the sun would come out and warm the countryside.

'Will you be all right from here?' the conductor asked. I knew exactly where to go. It wasn't far to the cousins' house but I was in no hurry and did not want to miss a thing. I was delighted with this new-found freedom. No one telling me not to dawdle; to keep up with the others. The primroses along the hedges were in full bloom. I loved their pale yellow colour. It was just right for spring. I picked a big bunch for Hannah and another for Cissie. She was the cross one and scarcely ever smiled. I would have to keep out of her way.

The lambs I had seen as babies had grown a lot. They were still in the field behind John Maguire's house. John himself came out to greet me.

'You'll be here for the Station Mass. It's the day after tomorrow. Hannah and Cissie have whitewashed the house inside and out. They have the place in tiptop shape.' I hadn't heard anything about the Station Mass. To tell the truth I didn't know what it meant. Hannah might have mentioned it to my mother on her last visit but I only listened when I wanted to hear. I walked on, wondering if we were going to the railway station, but that didn't make sense because we would have to go back into town to get the train. John had said something about whitewashing the house but then that was done every year. I'd just have to find out for myself.

When I came to Paddy and Mary's where the road forked, Mary was chasing the hens round the side of the house. She knew me well and I answered all her questions. She, too, mentioned 'The Station'.

'We had it here two years ago,' she said. From their house it was only a short distance to Hannah's. As soon as I came over the top of the hill I saw her standing in the middle of the boreen and waved to her.

'I saw the bus going down the tarred road and knew you weren't too far away.' As we went into the house she took the fresh soda cake from the windowsill where it had been left to cool. She talked about all the plans she had for that evening. We were to climb the hill behind the house, which we had often done on previous visits. From there we could see the lake and all the little houses dotting the countryside.

'We'll pop in to see old Pat too. He's on his own now and says he won't make it to the Station Mass. He's nervous in case he'd fall when he leaves his own place.' Hannah looked at me and saw the look of puzzlement on my face and the mystery was solved. Mass was to be celebrated in the house on Thursday morning. Hannah was in her element! It was an honour to have the priest come to the house, keeping up the old tradition of the Penal Days, when priests were forbidden to celebrate Mass. They had to move secretly from place to place for fear of discovery. I enjoyed the history lesson and as I drifted off to sleep that night, I wondered if Hannah's chattering upset Cissie, who had hardly spoken a word all evening, except to say that she hoped Thursday would be dry or the house would be ruined with the neighbours traipsing all over the place.

Next morning I awoke to a clatter of delph as Cissie made herself busy in the parlour. It was one of the rooms off the kitchen, only used on special occasions.

'And you're as well to go out and play when you finish your breakfast as I still have a lot to do. Jane is looking forward to spending the day with you. She'll be here any minute. I'll call the two of you for a bite to eat but don't let me see either of you in here until then.' I got the message! Jane lived further up the boreen and we always had great fun together. That day we could do as we wished from playing hopscotch, to paddling in the stream behind the barn and climbing trees we wouldn't have attempted under the watchful eye of Cissie. It was great! Occasionally Cissie appeared and we took no chances then. She was totally preoccupied with the task in hand, whether it was beating a rug or pegging clothes on the line.

I was invited to Jane's house for the evening tea and neither Hannah nor Cissie objected. I had often been to her house before but never for tea. We collected the eggs from the henhouse which her mother cleaned carefully before placing them in the big porringer on the hearth. She only boiled four eggs at a time; two for the older boys and two for her husband and herself. Jane and I played with the younger children in the yard until we were called in. Again there were four eggs in the porringer, two for Jane and me and two for the twins. We sat down at the scrubbed deal table and waited while Jane's mum washed some mugs and four teaspoons. Meanwhile the four younger children munched happily on slices of bread and butter while they waited their turn to eat. In our house there were six of us and we had eggcups and spoons. Somehow I knew that eggcups and spoons were not a priority in this house. Each time one group finished, the mugs and teaspoons were quickly washed in the basin of water that sat on the window ledge. I felt awkward as I tried to tap my egg on the table so that it sat right but Jane just smiled at me and gave it a single tap and it sat perfectly.

Hannah insisted that I go to bed early that night but not before she proudly turned the key in the parlour door and led me into the room to show me the table set for the Station breakfast.

Mass would be said in the kitchen and all the neighbours would attend but not everyone would be invited to stay for breakfast. Most of the men would slip quietly away to go back to their farm duties. They were glad of the excuse! They did not relish a morning in the company of the parish priest. He was a man who seized on any opportunity to get cheap labour; 'cheap' being no payment at all. They kept out of his way. Occasionally he resorted to getting at them through the women and then there was no way out. A few unfortunates among them would be unwilling volunteers by the time their wives got home that day.

The table was beautiful with all the best china set out; teacups with saucers and plates. Milk jugs and sugar bowls were beautifully arranged to show them at their best. Cissie's hand-embroidered tablecloth was a work of art and the colours complemented the blue, yellow and red of the china. The cloth had been lovingly washed, starched and ironed for the occasion.

In pride of place sat the beautiful set of silver cutlery, which had been a gift from the cousins in Philadelphia. Knives, forks and spoons adorned the table and put the finishing touches to the display. They were kept in a wooden mahogany box, called a canteen. It was lined in white satin, with individual compartments for each piece, which fitted like a glove into its designated place. The ornate lock had a small silver key which was kept in the Toby jug in the glass cabinet. I had seen it once before when I had eaten apple tart with one of the heavy spoons, a dessert spoon, Hannah had told me. The apple tart had tasted just the same as with an ordinary spoon, but it looked lovely and I was pleased to have been allowed to eat with it.

Mass next morning seemed to go on forever. The kitchen was packed as neighbours filed in with the menfolk standing outside the door. They preferred it that way and could safely have a bit of a chat with one of their friends without getting a dirty look from their wives. Two altar boys, glad of a morning off from school, were on their best behaviour. *'Introibo ad altare Dei'*...On and on it went until little by little the hard concrete floor began to take its toll on the women's knees. Their only hope was to lean back on their hunkers. Jane and I could not risk a chat with Cissie's eyes upon us. Father Andy preached a sermon and went on for a long time, reminding those gathered in the 'Lord's Name' of the importance of Station Masses in the life of the community. I liked listening to his voice when he led us all in 'Faith of Our Fathers'.

Finally, prayers were recited for all of the deceased relatives and friends, followed by a decade of the Rosary, with the 'Hail Marys' and the 'Holy Marys' overlapping more and more in a race to the final 'Glory Be'. It was over at last and with a sigh of relief all rose.

We piled into the parlour and the priest took his place at the head of the table. A second table of sorts was set up at the back of the room for the less important guests including the few children. A long plank of timber sat somewhat precariously on two porter barrels, long emptied of their contents, but a slight smell of alcohol still hung in the air. Another of Cissie's tablecloths covered the makeshift affair.

The breakfast was always the same. One or two slices of 'Shop Cooked Ham' (a rare treat) with one tomato cut in half on each plate. Nobody at our table got two slices! There were plates of soda bread and country butter, freshly baked scones and apple tarts too. Father Andy ate only one slice of ham and half a tomato. He might have preferred a boiled or poached egg but he wasn't given a choice. The ham and tomato was the staple diet at Station Masses even if it was served at 8.30 am. Father loved the scones and the apple tart. Hannah was proud as punch when he asked her what the secret was. She said that adding a yolk of egg to the pastry made all the difference. A few of the women still eating their ham and tomato smiled and took note. Their tarts would improve! It was a shame to see a whole slice of ham untouched on Father's plate but Hannah gave him a fresh plate, and on the pretext of wetting more tea, was seen to slip the holy slice among those that remained, carefully wrapped in greaseproof paper on the kitchen table. 'Waste Not Want Not.....'

Father Andy preached another sermon at the end of breakfast. Again he mentioned the importance of this occasion. Abundant graces would follow. I wondered if they would be a long time coming but didn't voice any opinion on the matter, partly because Cissie was again looking straight across the room at Jane and me. Maybe she would not be so grumpy when full of grace. Father proceeded to thank Hannah and Cissie for hosting the Mass and hoped that other neighbours present would put their names forward for the following year. That was the end of the Station.

When the priest left most of the neighbours left too. Only a handful of close friends remained. More tea was made and more apple tart was passed around. Then the job of cleaning up and washing up began in earnest. Tea towels made from the flour bags were handed out and we all helped. Cissie was the chief washer, while Hannah returned the good china to its resting place in the cabinet. The big white basin was filled and emptied, refilled and emptied several times and generous handfuls of washing soda were added. Cissie worked with furious speed and it was all we could do to keep up with her. The cutlery was piled on the kitchen table, where Hannah would shine it up, before replacing it in the mahogany box.

Next morning I would be going home.

The Communion Dress

It started out as the Communion dress but when Confirmation time came it was the Confirmation dress. Then it was all sorts; flower girl, concert and special occasions. It was most adaptable, solely out of necessity, because it served the same purpose for all the first and second cousins. Not one of us was the same size, but the dress went up, down, in, out and up and down again. It always ended up fitting the candidate like a glove! It was a much-travelled garment, having been to places we'd never seen, some cousins living as far away as Dublin and Kildare. Again, it was a case of up and down the country with Donegal, Fermanagh and Sligo/Leitrim most in demand. It was usually sent by bus, sometimes by train and was collected at the destination on arrival. The bus driver knew it well.

'Where's it off to this time?' he'd ask.

'Can't believe she's making her Confirmation. Sure she only made her Communion yesterday!'

But no matter where the dress went it always came back to roost in our house and remained on the top shelf of the wardrobe, where little hands could not reach. It was safe there. The box in which it was kept was a lovely golden colour and it was always carefully folded into its layers of white tissue paper. The first time I heard the poem *The Cloths of Heaven* by W.B. Yeats I immediately thought of the Communion dress. Why, I don't know, but it was a nice thought anyway!

The instructions sent by letter with the dress were always the same.

'Have a lovely day! Hope the weather keeps up. The shilling in the envelope is for her to buy a few sweets. Be sure to take the dress off as soon as she comes home. We'll need it here at the end of the month.'

We all longed for the day when we would wear it for our First Holy Communion. Being one of the youngest of the cousins I had to wait for what seemed forever but at last the day was near. Best of all was the trial run when out came the pins and thread and needles and even the measuring tape so as to adjust the length and breadth. Mother started early, at least one week before the big day, and several fittings were necessary as the changes were made. I just loved all the excitement around it. The first step was the laying out of the dress on the kitchen table to see if there were any marks or tiny stains that might have to be removed. There weren't any which immediately put my mother in a good mood.

'Well, at least they minded it,' she'd say.

As I looked at the dress laid out on the table, I took in every detail. I could admire it much better than when it was on me, but the pleasure of knowing I was to be the next person to wear it filled me with joy. I looked and looked. It was a bit like looking at a cake before getting a slice. As soon as the dress came out of the box the smell of moth balls was overpowering. They were permanently in residence in the layers of tissue and even topped up from time to time if the dress had not been in use. If three or four camphor balls were recommended, my mother felt that the baker's dozen would do the job twice as well!

Finally the dress was put on and I was lifted onto the table. Then the serious business of renovating the garment began. I had to keep still for what seemed like hours but I didn't mind. My mother held a host of straight pins in her mouth, between her teeth, and I watched as she released one or two as required. There was the occasional reprimand with,

'I told you not to move.'

'I'm sorry but my leg was itchy.'

'Now I'll have to start all over again.' And so it went on and on until we were happy that the dress was the right length and the cuffs on the sleeves had the pins in the correct position to allow for thinner wrists than those of the last model!

Then came the big day. The zinc bath was carried upstairs to the sitting room and large quantities of hot and cold water added from an array of saucepans and the two kettles. I had to endure being scrubbed from top to bottom until my body glowed. It was worth it all. The dress was hanging on the china cabinet and I knew I was almost there. Finally it was on! My mother hugged me and told me that I looked lovely and I could see that there were tears in her eyes. I knew I looked lovely. After all, I had waited for years to wear the dress. For several glorious hours I wore it. I enjoyed every moment and felt ten feet taller. Yes, I had to take it off sooner than I wished but I didn't protest. I knew the rules!

Then I had a second run, when the procession on Corpus Christi left from the Church grounds and we all walked down the street and back to the Church again. The first communicants had the honour of heading the procession and scattering rose petals as we went. We were pleased as punch, knowing that the other children were envious of us. In the church, on first Communion day, we had all been squashed into seats together and hadn't been able to admire each others' outfits. Now we were having a real fashion parade and we were revelling in it.

The singing was lovely and gave us the chance to chat a little as we scattered our rose petals.

'O Mary, we crown Thee with blossoms today.'

'Where did your mother get that lovely crown for your veil?'

'It's not a crown, it's a wreath.'

'Well, where did she get it anyway? It's lovely.'

'My aunt sent it from England.'

After what seemed a very short time we were almost back at the Church and the hymns were coming to a close with a lovely rendering of 'Hail Queen of Heaven'.

It was Confirmation however that posed problems. The cousins' height varied much more than it did at the first Communion stage. Some children seemed to sprout, while others remained small enough, but spread in a different direction! I had grown very tall, taller by far than any of my cousins. I was delighted with my new position as tallest but for the first time ever my mother was having difficulty in getting the dress to cover my knobbly knees. I didn't like being told that my knees were knobbly! That kind of language did not fit into the preparation for Confirmation. It wasn't very complimentary to my knees and I got quite upset. A frill at the bottom was suggested but one had already been added at some stage and another would be a different shade of white that would spoil the look.

'One way or another we'll hide your knees,' my mother promised. When I came home from school next day the kitchen was full of steam as she dampened the bottom of the dress and proceeded to apply pressure to the frill. She pressed it over and over again in order to stretch the material. I was afraid to watch and went outside until she announced that it was safe to come in and have a look. I had to admit that she had achieved a certain degree of success, but she was so intent on covering the knobbly knees, that she forgot to press the middle.

I smile as I look at the photograph. The knees are covered but the dress is up a fraction in the centre. Yes, I have kept the photograph (and the knobbly knees!) but I wonder who has the dress?

Aunt Bridget

The farm ran towards the foothills of the mountains which gave it protection from the north wind. It was known as a 'snug' farm, dry upland, ideal for producing cattle and sheep. It was here that his father had grown up with his siblings in the family home built by his grandfather in the late eighteen hundreds. The house had been enlarged over the years but was still not very big. When Hubert was getting married he decided to build a new house, about a hundred yards nearer the road, leaving his parents and his unmarried sister, Bridget, in the ancestral home.

Despite having her place in the home, Bridget was not happy with her lot. She no longer had control over any of the farm work, since the young bride, Moira, would be in charge of calves, poultry and all the things that had been hers. No one put pressure on her to leave but she was an independent type, set in her ways and had no intention of being an optional extra about the place.

She got a position as a priest's housekeeper in a nearby parish and took her job very seriously. Small in stature, she walked tall, conscious of her lack of height and in the process gave the impression of being rather pompous. The priest was an easygoing man, who went about his duties quietly and left the rest to Bridget. This may have been the reason why, little by little, she became very bossy and gradually took over a large portion of the Ministry (as she liked to call it), while the Reverend Father remained in ignorance of her changing status. Parishioners, who called to the door, were never allowed to see him without being first interviewed by the housekeeper. Most of them had to explain their reason for disturbing 'His Reverence'. If they were not prepared to do so they got a very frosty reception and were left standing, no matter what the weather, at the front door. Father O' Flaherty might have been the designated parish priest but Bridget was the real boss, with one exception. When travelling in the priest's car, he insisted that she sit in the back which was obviously a great disappointment to her. Only half of her face was visible as she strove to maintain an air of importance by stretching her neck upwards, looking directly at the road ahead.

When the elderly priest died and left Bridget a modest sum of money, she decided to give up work and to return to her old home, which she set about renovating to suit her needs. After a few months she moved in and she settled down in what was now a very comfortable, warm house. At first she was busy choosing new furniture and all the bits and pieces for the different rooms and she didn't spend much time with her brother's family, but when all was in order Aunt Bridget needed a new project and unfortunately for her nephews, they became her target.

A small path through the fields led from her house to theirs and visits to and fro became very frequent. She became even bossier, but the great thing was, that neither of their parents, Hubert or Moira, paid much heed to her. Her brother continued to call her Bridgie, a name to which she refused to respond, except by a sharp intake of breath, while their mother learned to deal reasonably calmly with various irritating remarks. One that rankled was

'I'll try to teach your children nice manners now that I've time.' On another occassion, after Hubert had carried out alterations to the sitting room, Bridget announced to Moira,

'Didn't you marry well!' This statement hurt their mother so much that she refused to talk to her for a few days. Even Bridget knew that she had gone too far and was a little more careful with her tongue from then on.

Hubert had always looked after both houses but now, as the boys were getting older, they were enlisted to do the odd jobs around Bridget's place. She never checked with any of them to see if they were available. Her word was their command. At weekends and holiday time, especially during the summer holidays, when the trout in the river were biting, she became even more demanding. Worst of all was the fact that she led them to believe she was really doing them a favour by keeping them suitably engaged.

'Send them over to me. I'll find something for them to do. It'll keep them out of mischief. Cathal, you can call over at ten past two, I'll have my lunch finished by then and you can mow the lawn and do a few other bits and pieces.'

The bits and pieces were what worried them most. They knew then that there was work to be done and errands to run. She even wrote out a list of all the jobs, keeping a copy for herself and that kept them on their toes. Each job, to be completed within a certain length of time, was neatly written on the list and there was no escape. If it wasn't done then it was simply transferred to the next day's assignment.

'When you've finished washing up those jam pots you could tidy the garage. You didn't do a great job last time.' As the jobs were completed she ticked them off. Bridget had taught them one valuable lesson for life:

'Do the job well the first time and you won't have to do it

again!' Despite her odd ways they actually liked going over to her house. It was a bit like owning a cross dog. If you behaved well and kept the house rules you got on fine.

She seldom entertained, for the very simple reason that she did not like having people around her. She confessed to their mother one day that people might consider her rather 'eccentric'. That was a new word that they had never heard and the youngest in the family piped up with

'Dad says that at times you can be a bloody nuisance with your airs and graces!'

'How was Bridgie today?' their mother would invariably ask, with a smile, on their return. 'Any lessons in etiquette?' Very often they wouldn't even remember what she had been saying. Some of her attempts to fill the gaps in their social education struck them as being funny.

'It's not "dinner" when you eat at midday. It's "lunch".' Despite her endeavours to convert them they still ate "dinner" in the middle of the day, when one of them would roar down the yard to their dad,

'Dinner's ready. Mum says to come at once when it's nice and hot.' Their mum's dinners were good and she cooked lovely scones and bread for the family but it was Bridgie who excelled in cookery. She made the most wonderful chocolate cakes, flapjacks, meringues and sponges, that never sank in the middle and just melted in the mouth. At the end of a work session the boys used to sit at the end of the kitchen table, while they savoured every mouthful of whatever was on offer. They didn't mind if the usual

'Don't stuff your mouth like that,' and other remarks came

heavy and fast. In fact they hardly heard her. The chocolate cake, in particular, was divine and they often pleaded with their mum to try to get the recipe. Nothing doing!

'Oh, I couldn't tell you. It's different every time. I could do it with my eyes closed.' Not one slice of cake or apple tart, or even a bun, was ever sent from her house to theirs. The food they were given was eaten at the kitchen table and remained a prisoner there.

It was when the letter arrived from America that the fun began. The cousins from Boston were coming to Ireland as part of their tour of Europe. They were seven in all. Bridgie refused to have them stay with her. She got her spake in early, with

'Naturally, it's with you, Hubert and Moira, they'll want to stay. I'll have them over for a nice meal the day they arrive. They can spend the whole evening with me and that will give you a break.'

The evening before the Yanks arrived Cathal called over on the pretext of seeing if help was needed. The news of her preparations had filtered through and he was secretly hoping she might try one of her recipes on him. The aroma of fresh home-baking wafted towards him as he opened the gate. His taste buds were on overdrive but it was dumb of him to think that he could fool his aunt. He was hastily dismissed with

'Not now, my dear. I'm up to my eyes,' and the door was firmly shut in his face. His pride was hurt and his stomach rumbled.

Imagine his surprise when he was called to the phone next morning.

'Was I wearing my glasses when you called yesterday?'

'I'm not sure because you closed the door so quickly.'

'You're not much help but maybe you'd come and help me look for them. I can't see well without them.' Cathal duly looked behind cushions, under chairs, everywhere in the kitchen, dining room and sitting room and even the bedroom, but to no avail. Then he thought of the bathroom. In his anticipation of at least a butterfly bun, if he could find the glasses, he accidently knocked a tumbler from the shelf onto the floor. It was no ordinary tumbler, but the one in which Bridgie kept a bottom plate of false teeth. They now grinned up at him in two pieces! No butterfly bun, just a torrent of abuse, a hasty dismissal with the final command,

'Shut the gate on your way out.'

He dried his tears and went home. Moira was on the phone, nodding sympathetically. No need to ask who was on the other end of the line!

'Don't upset yourself. These things happen. As soon as the Yanks leave, Hubert will take you into town to the dental mechanic and he will fix them good as new. Did you find the glasses? No! I'm sure they'll turn up.'

'What's up with her now?' asked Hubert as he came into the kitchen. Not sure of his reaction and close to tears Cathal told him the story.

'Sure she never wears her bottom teeth. The usual, she's making a federal case out of plucking a chicken.'

Next morning the visitors arrived, with Bridgie close on their heels. She was all smiles and held forth, in her best accent, on a number of topics. In the kitchen, before she left, she whispered to Moira,

'They are really nice and most cultured. As soon as I spoke

they knew I'd travelled.' Before she had left the parochial house she had gone on the diocesan pilgrimage to Lourdes! She was in a good mood now and before she left she turned to Cathal and Peter and said,

'Come over before the visitors and I'll have some jobs for you. Might even have some leftovers when we've finished our meal.' From that they knew that once again they were being confined to the kitchen.

That afternoon, as the visitors took their places at the dining room table, the chitter chatter reached the boys as they washed the good plates and stacked them carefully.

'On the pearl of your life don't let one fall. They belonged to your grandmother. Need I say more?' For some reason she was looking directly at Cathal. As the platters of cold beef, salmon and chicken were carried ceremoniously from the kitchen the two boys were kept in the kitchen washing the dishes. The carefully prepared salads then followed. The only contact they had was through the open door, from where they could hear the hum of voices and the occasional comment. Bridgie's rendering of Grace, in which she prayed for 'Distinguished Guests from Across the Sea', was nicely rounded off with '*Bon Appetit.*' She had surpassed herself and knew that the guests were impressed. Gradually, the chatter gave way to the sound of knives and forks on plates, as the visitors settled down to enjoy the meal.

Suddenly all hell broke loose. Voices were raised as one of the guests rushed from the room and hurried towards the bathroom. She had been last to help herself to the Caesar Salad. It was only when she felt the salad servers hit something hard at the bottom of the bowl that she looked in and saw a smiling plate of false teeth, adorned with small pieces of cucumber and tiny strips of lettuce and lemon, looking up at her. In her panic she let the server drop. It was then that she screamed and ran to the bathroom.

The boys knew that the game was up and made a hasty retreat. They had had their moment. The day of reckoning would come later!

Gone Fishin'

I never remember him as being young or old. He was always the same. In all the years I knew him he had never changed. He just seemed to go on forever, part of the everyday hub of the town, always there, except of course when you needed him urgently. Then he could be hard to find. He had a lisp all of his own. I could never fathom it! I tried hard but I could get nowhere near. We spent hours trying to imitate him, not in a nasty way, but out of sheer admiration. All to no avail! When we tired of other games we'd say

'Let's play Jack!' and off we'd go.

'I can't ssee anysing out of place, Ma'am' he'd say. 'It must be that bloody fusse again' or

'It'll have to be Thurssday, Misssus, I'm goin fissin to-day.'

He was an electrician by trade, I think, but I'm not even sure of that. The main thing was that Jack could do and did everything. He fixed electric kettles that had boiled dry, no automatic cut-off switch then.

'Which of them was it this time?' he'd ask, looking at each one of us in turn. He mended saucepans that never leaked again. He made his own fuses from an eternal supply of different bits of wire, in all the colours of the rainbow and more which he retrieved from the depths of his pockets. The extraordinary thing was that, without looking, he could pick out a piece in red, green or blue and he'd look at us and wink. We were speechless in our admiration! Maybe it was the weight of those two pockets that made him walk from side to side. What we would have given to get a right look inside! Instead we had to content ourselves with a view from without, as the various items emerged. A number of them went into his mouth as he sorted others out, whilst whistling a tune. The surprising thing was that he always found what he wanted. In later years he proudly carried a small box for the larger tools but the store in the pockets remained. There was no thrill in looking into the box, almost every house had its own, with a supply of screwdrivers, measuring tapes etc. But it was those pockets, carrying its treasure trove, that never failed to surprise. From its depths a 'Bulls-Eye' or two might appear or even a bit of a newspaper cutting. There were always several butts of pencils in a variety of colours. But the real butts were the ends of Woodbines, crushed, shedding whatever little tobacco they had once boasted but Jack didn't mind!

'A match, sonny, if you pleasse,' he'd say to my brother and all repairs ceased while he puffed on them, one by one, right down to the end. His fingers must have been heatproof, whether from his work or his smoking, or both. We felt sure that he could fix light bulbs that had blown, but he opted out on that one.

'Make me a cup of tea, sissy, and I'll have a look at the arm of that doll for you. Might be able to do something with it. Four ssugars and plenty of milk but don't sstir it.' I could never fathom why! Maybe it was the anticipation of savouring the thick, syrupy liquid at the bottom of the mug that prompted this remark. I just waited to hear the long, slow slurp that heralded the end of the drink. Meanwhile, the pieces of wire had been skilfully wrapped round the delph arm of the doll in record time. A job well-done of which any orthopaedic surgeon could be proud and which was sure to last.

He was a quiet man, small in stature, with a habit of stretching his neck as though it might make him look taller. I never knew where he lived, but he could be contacted by word of mouth.

'Did you see Jack?'

'Yes, he's up the town.'

'Tell him I need him in a hurry.' In record time he'd arrive at the door (if it wasn't a day for fishing). No callout charge for him. If it was a simple job he'd take no money, just the cup of tea and maybe,

'A few o' those lovely scones for me evenin' mug o' tay.' For anything else it was a matter of

'Whatever you think yourself, Ma'am.'

He was wholly at the mercy of the donor. Or maybe not. He was no fool! If the donation was not a fair one he was never to be put in a spot again. He'd always agree to come when sent for but simply didn't turn up.

'First thing tomorrow,' he'd say with a smile, but when the culprit was out of earshot he'd mutter,

'Tomorrow and tomorrow and tomorrow!'

He loved his fishing and for lengthy periods he would go missing. Money wasn't important but still he didn't seem short. In times of crises he'd never say an angry word but draw in his rod and respond to the call. I did notice, on a few occasions, that if you didn't know exactly where his favourite spot was, well hidden by a clump of bushes behind him, he would keep very quiet and ignore the caller. Who could blame him? Sometimes it worked.

'The main fuse has blown! Go and see if you can find Jack'. I hated being sent on the errand when we knew he was fishing. But then I might be lucky enough to see him catch a trout.

'How did you know you'd find me here?'

'I didn't, I just thought I'd look,' I lied.

'Pity you did,' he replied. 'They were biting well today.'

'Well, Jack! Did you find what's wrong?' asked my mother.

'Yes, Missus, A bloody mouse bit the wire.'

'Is he dead?' I piped up.

'Wouldn't you bloody well be dead if you ate it.'

It was the first and only time that Jack had ever raised his voice to me. The fishing must have been really good. Somebody else could call him next time. I'd be hiding too!

The Shadow of the Mountain

As the bus rounded the last corner, the town came into view. It was just as she remembered it; yet it seemed unreal, unfamiliar, rather like the experience of meeting someone you feel you've met before but you're not even sure. The mountain to the south, which she had often climbed as a child, formed a backdrop to the scene. Somehow it made her uneasy now. It seemed to tower over everything as though it were watching her. She had spent so much time as a child looking at it and marvelling at the changes brought about by the different seasons.

Often on Saturday mornings, when there was no school, she would drag the old rocking chair, that had been her Granny's, over to the window that looked directly on the mountain. She'd put her hands under her chin and stare out at it. She used to think that if she looked long enough she would see the colours changing. No matter how hard she tried she could never be a witness to the stealthy transformation that came so gradually, as if on tiptoe. Was the mountain mocking her, cheating her out of a wonderful experience?

Autumn time was her favourite, all those shades of russet, brown, yellow and mauve. In fact every shade imaginable could be gleaned from it if one tried hard enough. Often, as the year progressed, the mountain in its winter loneliness captivated her. She felt drawn to it almost as if it could talk. Now she looked at it and felt a kind of unease but could not figure why! As the winter sun shone on it, she could clearly see every little furrow and crevice, the same ones she had looked on all those years ago. That gave her some comfort. What had become of her sketch pad, she wondered, with all her drawings, particularly those with the wonderful vivid russet, orange and red symphony that was autumn and those others portraying so beautifully the lush green of summer?

Lost in her thoughts, she suddenly realised that the bus had stopped and the driver had spoken to her.

'Is this where you get off?'

'Yes,' she replied hurriedly and mother and daughter stepped down.

'This is it, Margaret!'

'Somehow I imagined it to be very different but I recognise the mountain you often talked about Mum. It's just as you described it. Where do we go now?' Margaret asked.

'I think we should have something to eat. We haven't had anything since early morning,' her mother replied. She needed time to prepare, to brace herself and above all to come to terms with her past.

'Do I know you?' asked the white-haired lady in the restaurant as Mary stood at the till to pay.

'Your face looks vaguely familiar. You're not from around here, are you?'

'No, I'm not,' she said as her eyes met her daughter's. Mary had already recognised Brigid Deery, who had been running the restaurant for as long as she could remember. Now was not the time for talk!

'You knew that lady, Mum! Why did you pretend you didn't?'

'That was a long time ago, Margaret. It belongs to the past.'

The flower shop was where the old chemist's premises had

been; such a kind man, always asking how her mum's asthma was behaving, while unscrewing the top of the sweet jar and reaching into its depths to retrieve a long black liquorice stick which he always gave her. She wondered where he was now, probably long since dead.

'I'll take two dozen of those red roses,' she said. Then, mother and daughter made their way up the hill to the little cemetery which lay in the shadow of the abbey. It was a while before they found the grave. The headstone simply stated:

To The Memory of Margaret Mahon
Died Nov 1965
Her husband, Patrick Mahon
Died Dec 1973

That was all! He had always been a man of few words.

Suddenly, it all came crowding in on her. Her mother and herself whispering in the kitchen, when he had gone upstairs. He was a good man but set in his ways. She was the apple of his eye and in his own simple way he had great plans for her.

'When you get your exams you'll be fit for any position, the Bank maybe, or you might even like to go to University. Wouldn't it be great to have a steady job!' and he'd look at her, his only child, with eyes full of love and expectation.

That had all changed.

'What will you do now?' her mother asked.

'I'll go away for a while,' she answered. They had both cried.

'It's a lovely place to rest, Mum,' Margaret said, as she gently laid the flowers on the grave. Mary felt her throat tighten. How she loved her daughter, so sensitive and caring! Already, Margaret was growing into a beautiful young girl. She had sensed how difficult this was for her mother and was doing her very best to support her. It was she who had suggested that her mum should go back once more. They had gone through a lot together.

Mary remembered the morning she had spoken to her father. It was a Saturday, wet and miserable and the mountain was covered in a heavy, dense mist. It seemed to be in keeping with her own low spirits, as she stared out of the kitchen window trying to find the right words. Maybe she had been too forthright. But that was the way he had always wanted it.

'Tell the truth straight out. No waltzing about. Get to the point.'

When she blurted out,

'Dad, I've something to tell you. I'm pregnant.' She waited but no words came. Instead, a terrible look of disbelief and disappointment gave way to a frozen, cruel mask of horror on his face.

'I'm sorry, Dad, I really am. What am I going to do?' There was complete silence for what seemed an eternity but could only have lasted seconds. His words, when he spoke, hit her like ice-cold steel. Turning towards her mother, who was nervously drying her hands on her apron, he asked,

'Have you seen my cap lying around?' and without waiting for a reply he walked straight to the chair where he always left it, went out the door towards the farmyard and out of her life. She had left that evening before he was due back. She could never forget the look of hurt on his face.

As Mary knelt with her daughter in the wintry sun and tried

to pray, the loneliness of those first months and years in England was foremost in her thoughts. She had phoned home a number of times and it was always her mother who answered. Sometimes, it just rang out and when it did she knew her mother was not there. She had spoken to her just a week before Margaret was born.

'Don't worry about your dad. He'll come round once the baby is born.'

The morning the baby arrived, Mary had cried tears of joy and sadness. What she would have given to have had her parents by her side! There were a lot of visitors to the ward but if the other mothers noticed anything unusual in the fact that she never mentioned the child's father, or her own parents, they asked no questions. She could have made excuses about a husband abroad for work and parents back in Ireland, unable to travel. Instead she held her head high and made no apology to anyone for the beautiful little daughter that was hers. She was determined to get on with the business of rearing her child on her own.

Two days before leaving hospital she decided to ring home. The corridor was noisy with early morning activity as she dialled the number. The phone rang for some time before a voice answered.

'Yes?' Mary immediately recognised her father's voice.

'Dad, it's me.'

'How did you hear?'

'Hear what?'

'That your mother died and was buried a week ago.'

She could never recall the rest of the short conversation except that he had asked her not to come home. He had enough trouble as it was! The time was not right. It was later in the day that she suddenly remembered he hadn't given her a chance to tell him he had a granddaughter. That was the last she had heard from him. Once or twice she had tried phoning but there was no answer. She had given up but had never forgotten. Each Christmas she sent a card with a photo of Margaret and included her home phone number in the envelope, but had never received a reply. The hurt she had carried for over twelve years weighed heavily upon her. How could he have turned his back on his only daughter and granddaughter, but then she knew, better than anyone, that he was a proud man who didn't forgive easily.

The old neighbour stared in disbelief as she recognised her at the door.

'Mary, it's yourself and this must be your daughter. I recognise her from the photographs. Come in, she's the picture of her Granny, God rest her. How are you at all! It's been a long time.' Poor old Mrs Mc Hugh was lovely as ever, showing no embarrassment or awkwardness, as she welcomed them into her warm kitchen, where she busied herself wetting tea in the big old brown pot that Mary remembered so well.

'What a pity it took me so long to find your phone number. There it was, after all this time, tucked in the back of the photo of you and Margaret. He kept them all on his bedside locker. I remember well the day he died. He must have slipped quietly away after finishing his dinner. I always checked on him before I went to bed. At first I thought he had just fallen asleep but when I saw the dirty dishes on the table I knew something was wrong.'

He had been dead for over four years before she heard the news. By then she had a good job, was well paid and with her young daughter had settled down to a relatively comfortable life in London.

Lost in her thoughts, Mary suddenly realised that Mrs Mc Hugh was still talking, bringing her up to date on the whereabouts of friends and neighbours. She felt much better by the time she said goodbye to the old family friend, with promises to keep in touch and half-promises to come back on holiday at a later date.

'We'll make another quick visit to the grave, Margaret, if that's all right with you.'

'Of course, Mum. I'd like that.'

They set off up the hill again. By then the slanting, watery sun had taken on a hue of pale pink. A light wind began to scurry around them and the small headstones offered no protection. The sun came out for a few brief moments casting a slanting light on the mountain behind and a weak ray of sunshine fell on her parents' tombstone. It would soon be dark. Already the mountain was bathed in shadow. Mary looked again at the simple grave, now adorned with red roses.

The sun lowered gradually in the sky and a few leaves went dancing playfully between the paths. It was time to leave. As mother and daughter walked arm in arm down the path, a lone robin alighted on the grave of Margaret and Patrick Mahon and chirped a brief, solitary evensong by way of farewell. They both turned to look and their eyes met. Darkness was quickly falling and the hush of evening was broken once more, this time by the voice of the young girl, as she quietly took her mother's arm and said

'Mum, let's go home.'

The Removal

'I suppose we'll have to give John a lift. He didn't give us much choice.'

'That's why he phoned,' Martin replied. 'We haven't heard from him since Pat Mc Daid's funeral.'

The old cousin, Michael Joe, had died and once again the family duty of attending the removal and funeral had to be honoured. Janice had never met him but, from the moment she had married Martin and come to live in the area, she resigned herself to the importance of funerals for the whole extended family and the local community. The last thing she wanted was to spend the weekend going to another removal, followed by the funeral the following day. She would meet the same group of people, most of whom she did not even know. That was bad enough but to have to tolerate John for both trips was just too much. He seemed to take a special delight in sickness and death! These, she had decided, were his social life. Her plans for a weekend in Galway, with a bit of retail therapy thrown in, would have to wait.

Needless to say, John accepted the offer. As far as he was concerned it was only right that his first cousin's son should be available, whenever he needed to pay his last respects to the few remaining relatives and friends, when they passed away. He had been much more attentive before getting in with that 'wan' from Dublin. It was only after her arrival that Marty had stopped bringing him for his pension of a Friday, mumbling some excuse about being 'tied up'. He had tied himself up all right! John had never graced them with a visit from the day he had married her, nor had he been asked. When it came to funerals he suited himself. He was no longer able for more than a few miles on the bicycle and it was nice to have the bit of a chat with Marty. He was a nice young man even if he'd made the mistake of going far afield to find a woman. They'd live to regret it. For one thing he wasn't going to leave the pair of them anything. The only pity was that he'd had to hire a hackney car to go into the solicitor's to change his will. The car cost plenty and so had the solicitor. There was nothing he could do about it. That lassie would have smelled a rat if he'd asked Marty to drive him. Anyway, the two of them had good jobs and from what he could gather from the neighbours, they spent money as if it was going out of fashion.

He settled himself into the back of the big car, a Merc, he was told! All he wanted was a safe trip in any make of a car as long as it had a good engine and four wheels. He had already decided he wouldn't engage in much conversation and for the first few miles remained silent. But he couldn't keep it up. Being a lonely man, living on his own, with only a good neighbour or two popping in for a chat, giving or getting a bit of news, his opportunities were few and far between. Bit by bit his resolve weakened. The car was warm and comfortable and he decided to make the most of the trip even though the pair weren't making much of an effort to entertain him, apart from the Dublin lassie asking him how he was keeping.

'I'm fine but I'm a bit concerned about the time. Will we get there before the hearse comes down the road, Marty?' She answered for him.

'Of course we will. Martin knows exactly how long it will take.' So he was Martin now. More of her nonsense!

'I know this whole area like the back of me hand.' That was the start! They took it in turns to reply to the barrage of questions and comments that came with the speed of a shotgun. Most of the time he ignored Janice, occasionally addressing her as Missus and after that she decided to ignore him. Not that he seemed to notice. In fact, he didn't need answers. He had the solution to every topic!

'Does your father's nephew still live in Ballymoe? Ah, I remember now that he never moved to the bungalow his sister gave him on the upper road. Did you know Missus, seein as you're not part of the family, that most of those cousins emigrated to the States years ago. He stayed and never married, which was no loss, because he was a useless, lazy lump, who never did a thing to that house from the time his poor mother, God rest her, passed away. That must be ten year ago or more. It's a pity ye didn't take the lower road, Marty, till we'd have a chance to see how the place looks now. I think ye were foolish goin this way; it has to be longer and I'm still thinkin we're goin to be late, but far be it from me to tell ye yer business. Many's the time I cycled out here of a Sunday when I was a young lad but I'm looking now at all those fine houses closed up. There was ten of a family in that one just comin up. Do ye hear me, Marty? Ye must have heard your father mention Johnny Mac's family. He was a bit fond of the sup but the wife was a great wee woman; no time in those days for high falutin notions like they have nowadays. The farms were small but ye could grow plenty to keep the house goin and there was always enough bacon to go round. I don't know what's goin to happen to the small farmers now. Yon boys in Brussels have the thing backways; they're payin them now not to grow anything. Sure how could that work! Is it the language that's the problem? Maybe they made a mistake in the translation or something. I don't know, but what do those boys with the stiff collars and fancy ties know about the West of Ireland? Mind you our own boys in Leinster House don't do a lot for us either. Do you see the ruins there on your left? We used often have a game of football at the back of that house and I can still get the smell of the soda bread Mrs Hannigan baked for us, lovely big slices with the homemade butter and blackcurrant jam. Do ye make any jam, Missus? That's another thing about the Brussels Boys. Ye can't make your own butter any more to sell to the shops and still young boys are being paid to play football. There's no sense to it all. I don't know what the world's comin to or where it's goin to end.'

In one last great effort to liven up the conversation and to make Janice a bit more comfortable, Martin pointed to a number of new houses along the road and even named some young people, who had returned to the countryside, working in town and doing a bit of farming on the side. A big change, all agreed on that one. In vain! Had he listened at all?

'I'm surprised they're still able to keep a priest in this end of the parish. There is only a handful of small farmers out here and I don't know how they're surviving. Do you see that little house on yer left, Marty? That's where Mrs Regan reared eight children all on her own after her husband was killed off the tractor. Very sad, the youngest was only a baby. Not that he was much of a farmer; his eldest son runs the farm now and is a credit to his mother. She was the woman that could bake the best currant bread in the parish but nobody ever got the recipe.

"Just a bit o' this and a fistful o' that" she'd say with a smile.

Hers was the best bacon and cabbage too but that was something we all got too much of in our youth. Tell the truth I'm not fond of it and when the American cousins treated me to me dinner at the Airport last year, I declare to God the special of the day was, guess what! Bacon and Cabbage. Are ye sure we haven't passed the turn for the Church, Marty? I didn't think it was this far out.'

'No, we haven't. It's beyond the school and the security lights there are a good pointer.' He was off again.

'I declare it's a disgrace, having to get security lights. The young ones nowadays get free schooling and some of them can think of nothing better than to break in at night and destroy all before them. That's the only interest they have in education. The whole world is upside down. The...'

He stopped suddenly as they finally turned up the narrow road towards the Church. Silence prevailed and soon they reached the point where the road branched off with a sign 'R.C. Church'. Progress was slow as the road narrowed to a grassy lane. A short distance ahead the funeral cortege was making its way up the hill, followed by a long line of cars and bicycles. A number of people were walking directly behind the hearse. The whole procession moved at a snail's pace and very soon other cars joined the long queue. They all stopped as the coffin was lifted out and carried inside the Church. Bicycles and cars were abandoned, as people hurried with heads down and shoulders hunched against the sharp frosty air. The Church bell rang in sombre tones. John had become silent except for the few quiet words spoken as he got out of the car.

'I knew we were cutting it too fine.'

He was afraid he'd miss out on any of the proceedings. As

the three walked together in welcome silence, the countryside all around was bathed in the light of a new moon, casting eerie shadows on fields already white with frost. The night air was cold and crisp, with a myriad of golden stars, dotted against the background of a dark blue sky. Janice held her breath, as the beauty of the early night enveloped her. She was glad she had come. Somehow, she felt a sense of belonging as they arrived at the Church. Mourners were shuffling into pews, some anxious to find a seat near the back, from where they could observe, and mentally record all who attended and to note in particular those who hadn't come. It would be a topic of conversation around the firesides until the next parishioner's passing took over.

Janice reluctantly took leave of the idyllic night scene as she followed Martin and John into the Church porch, joining the large crowd, all with one purpose in mind, to get inside before the prayers began; mourners united in grief for a short period as the finality of another death in their community was driven home. The bell struck again in single peals, until its solemn tones were almost drowned out by the barking of a dog, disturbed from its sleep by an unfamiliar intruder.

The Church was now filled to capacity and still they came, men, women and children, pushing and shoving their way into seats already full, whose occupants had no alternative but to make room for them. The poor unfortunates at both ends held on for dear life, with one leg dangling precariously into the aisle It was important for those who were there to be seen and to meet in person the chief mourners.

Finally, the prayers were over and the crowd waited expectantly for the priest to make the first move. He was a tall man and had acquired the habit of bending down to place his left hand on the shoulder of each of the relatives in turn, but shaking hands only with the principals. It was a well-practised ritual. Death had become all too familiar to him and he would, no doubt, repeat the performance on a number of occasions before the winter was out. He could only hope that the weather would hold for the burial the following day; the bout of pneumonia last winter had left him tired and spent.

His exit was the signal for the congregation to approach the front rows, where the bereaved sat in a huddled bunch, already anticipating a few hot whiskies or a cup of tea later on. It would be a long night as neighbours and friends sat together. For now, they knew that most of those in the rows behind would not leave until they had spoken to each one of them, some of whom would take the opportunity of asking:

'And who is this then?' and the cousin from England or Scotland was identified and named. Meanwhile the crowd waited patiently, some not so patiently, as the relatives did the customary thing of taking the hand that was offered and thanking each individual as they filed past.

It was late when the threesome finally bade goodnight to the family of Michael Joe. In spite of her earlier misgivings Janice had enjoyed the trip. She had never felt like this before; and suddenly she realised that she was glad to be a part of it all. The kindness of all those to whom she had been introduced had been very touching. There was a sincerity and warmth in their greeting.

Martin drove home in silence. Even John seemed to welcome

the quiet hum of the engine as they neared the familiar landmarks of their homes. Almost in a whisper as though talking to himself he spoke.

'He'll be missed. Too many of the old friends have passed away. It's fierce lonesome sometimes on my own. There's days when I don't see a sinner.' Suddenly Janice understood. The old man was feeling sad. As they neared the lane that led to John's house she turned to him and said,

'Would you like a cup of tea before you go home? Martin will drop you off later.' Over the cup of tea and a ham sandwich he came into his own and spoke of the Christmas morning when he and the deceased had set out for the early Mass, fasting of course, with the stars still bright in the sky. Sitting at the kitchen table Janice drank in every word. She knew now she'd fit in and she met Martin's eyes with a smile.

'Thanks Missus for the tea. I'll see ye in the morning and you and me can have a good chat.' Looking directly at Martin with a broad grin he announced,

'Ye're a fair judge of a woman! Now ye need to pick me up early because there'll be a fierce crowd and I want to see it all.' As he lowered himself into the front seat beside Martin, he held the door ajar to wish Janice 'Good Night' and again with a smile and a nod of his head announced

'Ye know something....... it's hard to beat a good funeral!'

Boots

'Do they fit?' asked the assistant in a posh accent.

'Perfectly, but I am not prepared to spend two hundred and fifty euro on a pair of boots. I thought there was a sale on at the moment.'

'She is looking for something less expensive,' said my daughter. The assistant looked at me with a bored expression as she gazed out the shop window.

'Try these. They may suit you. They're not great quality but they'll probably last the season. They're only thirty-five euro.'

She looked at me again with that bored expression. I wondered if she thought I might only last another season too!

The afternoon was warm for late autumn and I was beginning to feel tired. We had spent the day shopping, or rather my daughter had. My function had been to hold several garments, the ones that might do, if she couldn't find the 'one' she really wanted. I was definitely wilting and badly needed a cup of tea. All I wanted was a pair of boots but I wanted a bargain. Sitting down on a little footstool I decided that the thirty-five euro ones were worth a try. They were narrow, in simulated black skin, (in other words plastic) at the right price. My daughter's enthusiasm was infectious.

'I'll help you put them on, Mum.' Pulling them up was difficult but finally I stood up, walked to the mirror and looked down. Was I pleased! The boots hugged my calves like a glove. I'd be the height of fashion. Just like a young one! I might even get an invite to mount the catwalk in the next local fashion show. However, when I looked up to survey the whole 'me' in the mirror and saw my pale face with the puffy, tired eyes I abandoned that thought. The combination of face and feet and the middle bit with the bulge (just at the point where they all met) weren't sending out the right signals. No miracle there! Anyway I was going to settle for the boots. What harm if they were too young looking for me! There was no law against it.

'Do you want the box for them, pet?' So I was 'pet' now.

'To whom are you speaking, my dear?' I replied. The cheek of her, not half my age.

'No' I replied, 'a bag will do nicely.'

'No exchange without the box,' she said. Why would I want to change them? They were such a bargain.

Back home in my own house, I carefully put my new boots in the wardrobe. I was saving them for that special occasion, when all heads would turn to look at me. I was meeting the usual group on Tuesday morning, so on my way to bed on Monday night I couldn't resist the temptation to try them on one more time. They were gorgeous. I slipped one foot in, or rather tried, but made very little progress. I slid my leg into the boot but my heel got stuck and refused to budge. It would not sit into its designated area. It had fitted perfectly before and it would just have to do so now. I pulled the boot up but it didn't move an inch and my leg didn't move down an inch so I resorted to pushing my heel down, panting and puffing and even swearing now and then. Nothing seemed to work. Then the dreadful thought struck me. Had that girl given me the wrong size? I checked it on the freestanding left one, which had toppled over and didn't look quite as elegant as it had on the stand in the shop. Wrong on that one! Size 6 was right. Then it dawned on me. I was now wearing cotton socks. When I had fitted them on in the store I had been wearing none. I'd try once more without the socks. That should work. Still a struggle! As I shoved and pulled once more I took comfort in the thought that last winter had been very mild. Maybe this one would be too. Who'd need socks? One last pull before settling down for a good night's rest. It was then that I felt the pain in my shoulder. I must have pulled something.

By morning nothing had changed, except that the pain in my shoulder was worse. The boots were still the same size and my feet were no smaller. I had hoped that after a good night's rest they might have shrunk. Maybe pop socks would work. My neck was really hurting but I decided to have another try. There were holes in the toes of the new pop socks now, but I wasn't giving in. Neither were the boots. I'd just have to resign myself to the fact that they would have to be worn without socks. I finally came up with a plan. I eased my left foot into the boot. I gently wriggled my toes to the top while the boot collapsed but I felt I was getting there. All this pushing and shoving wasn't doing my shoulder any good. I stopped to get my breath and to admire my purchase. Those boots were a real bargain! Just then I noticed the little tear that had appeared in the spot where I had forced the boot to meet my ankle.

I phoned the girls. Sorry I couldn't meet them after all. Something had come up. Or was it down! I was getting confused. Why did that rhyme about the 'Good Old Duke of York' keep coming into my mind? My appointment with the doctor was for 4.30. I'd better hurry. I had it all worked out now, allowing a good five minutes to get my feet where I wanted them, in the boots!

'What have you been up to?' asked the doctor. (Please, no

more up or down!)

'Have you been lifting again?'

'No, just pushing,' I replied. He looked at me with a 'No Further Questions' attitude and nodded sympathetically. I saw him add a little footnote to my chart.

Going to a doctor is an expensive business nowadays! I paid forty-five euro there and then I was off to the pharmacy with the prescription. It came to sixty-five euro for two weeks' supply of anti-inflammatory pills and then there was the tablet for the tablets.

'I love your boots,' the assistant volunteered as she handed me my change.

'Thanks,' I beamed, 'they were a real bargain.'

I met her again, after my second visit to the doctor.

'Still wearing those lovely boots,' she smiled. 'Indeed I am,' I said proudly.

The boots have served me well during this rather cold winter. The doctor keeps asking me if I'm wearing warm enough clothes. Of course I am. I'm a sensible woman. It's only my feet that feel a bit cold now and then, but it's a price I was willing to pay for beauty! I wonder if I will be as lucky this year in the January Sales!

The Venture

It was the perfect solution to our cash flow problem. We hadn't a penny left. Saturday's pocket money had all been spent and the last showing of *'The Wizard of Oz'* in the local cinema was only one day away. No loans no matter how we pleaded! But now, at least, we had a plan, carefully drawn up, the figures all done. We were ready.

They were all washed, looking spick and span, standing in neat rows in perfect symmetry. Only the final touches were needed to make them look even better. We matched like with like and that was it; a job well done! In all, we had gathered three dozen quality jam pots for sale!

My sister had volunteered to do the talking, speech well-rehearsed, while I had the job of introducing the merchandise. Our first hurdle was to get out of the house without being seen. We hadn't sought sanction for our project. No plan had been submitted to higher authority for approval. It made sense to hold our fire until we could show the fruits of our enterprise. It was better not to tempt fate. When successful we could present our findings and be commended for our initiative. For now, discretion was the greater part of valour. Information imparted would only be on a need to know basis.

First port of call was the 'Cake and Jam Shop'. The party line was delivered;

'We thought you might like to have some clean, empty jam pots, all in perfect condition.'

'You are very kind. I could do with half a dozen. I'll take some more later on if you have any left.' I was absorbed in admiring a beautiful cream and jam sponge on the counter. Maybe we would collect enough money to come back and buy that sponge and still have enough left to go to the cinema. I could taste the jam and cream and see us both sharing the cake with Mum. She wouldn't have the heart to refuse permission to go to the film, since we'd have earned the money ourselves. I was lost in thought, when a pinch from my sister jolted me back to the job in hand. I carefully handed over the merchandise, six pots, uniform in size. They were the best six pots in the lot. We were off to a flying start.

'I'd like to give you something for your thoughtfulness.' My eyes were focused on the sponge cake. I hesitated for a moment before pointing to the cake but by then it was too late. Perhaps the lady had not seen the longing on my face or perhaps she had. I don't know how she could have missed it! She steered us to a basket on another table, near the counter, where a nicely printed notice proclaimed:

Yesterday's Bake
Today's Take
All Half Price

With one hand on each shoulder she led us towards the basket, full of scones, and handed one to each of us. We hated raisins! I followed my sister out onto the street. Maybe I had missed something!

'How much did she give you?'

'Nothing, just nothing!' I tasted the scone, avoiding a raisin. It was horrible. We both dropped the scones into the bag along with the jam pots.

Still, we had six more shops on our list. Things could only get better from here on. We went to a grocery shop which had a huge display of oranges in the front window. A neatly written sign in big bold letters proclaimed

'Remember the Sick'

We were more hopeful on seeing the notice, though I don't know why. We weren't ill but my tummy didn't feel the best. Still, it would all be fine when the money was safe and sound in our pockets. Into the shop we went, with the bag of jam pots and approached the owner, Tony, who was behind the counter, elbows resting, as he read the newspaper. His wife was nowhere to be seen. She was usually there on her own, but when both of them presided, we always made straight for her. Ice creams were bigger when she cut them from the block. She was the one who often stuck half a 'Flake' at the top and, when handing it across the counter, covered it discreetly with her hand so that 'His Lordship' did not see it. I had a strange foreboding that things were not going according to plan but we did our best. Speech delivered! Result: two manky oranges with soft skin added to the collection in the bag! Not only that, he had the cheek to take a dozen and a half of our pots saying

'I'll relieve you of six more to lighten the load. That bag is too heavy for youngsters like you to be carrying.'

Next stop was the chemist's. The lady there knew us well and asked how we were all getting along, what classes we were in and finally the same speech was delivered with more or less the same result; a bar of 'Knight's Castile' soap for our mother. Mum would be pleased but that was no help to us. The real problem now was that we had only six pots left and not one penny in our pockets. What's more my two arms were sore from carrying the bag. I never thought jam pots could be so heavy. What puzzled me was the fact that Tony didn't even give us tuppence. My father had always said that he was 'Tight as Tuppence' and the fact that his wife was one of mother's best friends seemed to make no difference.

The next two shops said they were not interested. This was even worse! As we were passing the shoemaker's I turned and made a dramatic entrance by falling over a pair of boots on the floor. It was so dark inside that I couldn't see a thing. I had dropped the bag and there was no mistaking the sound of broken glass. My sister was furious.

'What were you doing, coming in here? Sure Pat the Cobbler doesn't need jam pots.'

'He does when he goes fishing.' Pat got a shovel and started picking up the glass that had scattered everywhere.

'What are you doing with jam pots?' he asked. My sister was sulking. It was all too much for me.

'We were trying to get the money to go to the pictures by selling jam pots but we haven't got a penny.'

By the time we left Pat's we had both cheered up. The feed of 'Custard Creams' and lemonade had revived us and we had one shiny new sixpence between us. Surely our mother would give us the extra sixpence. We could get an advance on next week's pocket money and do a whole lot of extra jobs.

Dragging our legs home, and with three pots still in the bag (one with a bit of a crack), we stole in by the back door. Mother was in the kitchen.

'Where were you girls?' Without waiting for a reply she added, 'Never mind now! There's work to be done. Bring in all the jam pots you can find in the garage and start washing them. It's time to make the blackcurrant jam. I have all ready. All I need now are the pots.'

How much jam would fit in three pots, one of them cracked?

The Field

The big meadow was right beside the house. As he left for work each morning he never glanced in its direction, but could still feel its hold over him after all the years. As far back as he could remember that field had been his kingdom. It was there with his father, Mike, that he had taken his first steps. When he was older he kicked his ball there. Being an only child, he spent hours on his own playing games, fighting mighty warriors and ruling the world. As soon as he came home from school he'd throw down the schoolbag, cross the gate and run to find his father. It was his little world which he thought would never change.

For a time nothing did change. But, bit by bit, he could sense that something was wrong. He chose to ignore what was happening, because he did not understand any of it. His father didn't seem to laugh or even talk to him as he had always done. When he asked him if he had a cold coming on he smiled, put his hand on his shoulder and said,

'I'll be fine. Just a bit of a headache.' He wanted to believe him, but in bed at night, when his parents thought he was asleep, snatches of conversation from the kitchen, below his bedroom, disturbed him.

'Not able to pay the bills... another letter from the bank today... we just can't go on.' His mother's voice trying to calm him.

'We'll manage somehow. Things will get better.' Of course they would. Maybe he had been dreaming and none of what he had heard was true. He wouldn't think about it anymore. That way it would go away and when he sat under his tree in the field all was well again.

As he returned from school one day, he met an ambulance as it drove off down the laneway from the house. All he could think of was his granny. Was she sick or even dying? He ran towards the house and into the hallway, where neighbours were speaking in low tones. What were they doing there? They turned to look and made way for him.

'What's wrong and where's Granny?' He could not believe his eyes when Granny rushed out from the kitchen and took him in her arms. Her eyes were full of tears as she whispered,

'I'm so sorry, Colm. It's your Dad; he's gone to heaven.' The voice went on,

'Mum's in the ambulance with him now but it's too late. There was nothing that could be done to save him.' It couldn't be. Just that day in school the teacher had said that when you were good God looked after you. He tried to say something but the words would not come. His mouth was frozen. He broke free from his grandmother's arms and ran outside, past the line of neighbours, who again made way for him and he raced down to the meadow, threw himself on the ground beneath his tree, and sobbed his little heart out. He stayed there until his mother came to find him when she returned from the hospital.

Weeks and months passed and First Communion came and went. He prayed hard to God to give him back his dad. He would explain the miracle, just like Lazarus. But nothing happened. Still, he didn't give up. The summer holidays were coming and he would sit under his tree and pretend. If he pretended hard enough and closed his eyes really tightly his dad would be there when he opened them. At least it was worth a try. The prayers hadn't worked.

The last day of school was Sports Day and he was determined to beat Joey Kelly in the race. His father would be so proud. He did beat Joey who was furious and turned to him in anger.

'You're a freak just like your dad. Everyone knows that he hanged himself from the tree in your field.' He raced home…surely it wasn't true!

'Joey said dad hanged himself.' His mam's eyes told him it was true. He felt so old for his seven years and from that day on he never mentioned his father and he never went to the meadow.

They said time was a great healer. He'd get over it. In a way maybe he had. He fell in love with Mary Smith and married her. Now they were expecting their first child. Still, his mother worried about him, as did Mary. She tried to talk to him about what had happened, but he always brushed it aside with

'I don't want to talk about it. That was a long time ago.' His mother, Anne, told Mary, that after that first terrible day, he had never shed a tear. The two women knew, that after all that time, a great sore was still festering within him. Mary tried to ignore the mood swings, occasional outbursts of anger and his cynicism. She wondered how long they could go on together and now that her first child was about to enter the world she became more and more anxious.

……………..

He hurried into the hospital ward and then he saw her. In her arms was a tiny bundle. It was all over. As he lifted his tiny infant son, with the little screwed up face, the tiny perfect fingers grasped his. Something gave way inside him and he felt a huge lump in his throat. A surge of emotion rose from within but he still resisted the urge to shed a tear.

Soon Mary and the baby were home and Colm set about helping in any way he could. He was very proud of the fact that he was the one who could wind the baby, when even his mother failed. He had softened somewhat but the wall of silence remained. Anne mentioned his father in passing once or twice but she could see the hard line of his jaw become taut. She had hoped that the baby's arrival would have taken care of everything, now that he too had become a father. No name had been chosen and it would soon be time to organise the Christening. The infant was simply referred to as 'baby'. The women knew that Colm needed to deal with what had happened.

Two weeks after the birth, Mary was rushed to hospital. Once again an ambulance drove down the narrow boreen. She had lost consciousness before leaving the house. Colm, who had lost his father so tragically twenty years before, was now faced with the prospect of losing his wife too. As he drove in pursuit of the ambulance reality finally struck. His selfishness, self-pity and anger all rose before him. For the first time, he realised that the pain and suffering he had endured had also been experienced, not only by his mother, but also by his granny, now long since dead. He had done nothing to help them. He felt ashamed as the tears coursed down his face and he could feel their saltiness in his mouth.

'Please, God, let Mary live and give me a second chance,' he prayed as he ran in the hospital door, unaware that he was repeating the same words out loud to all those around him. He hurried into the Intensive Care Unit where he watched her fight for her life. He sat by her side holding her hand. He could no longer resist the wave that unleashed the huge sobs that were released from his chest. He cried as he had never cried before. He wondered if Mary could hear him. Over and over he told her how sorry he was.

She remained in a critical condition for another three days and then began to recover slowly. When she finally opened her eyes and looked into his, she could see the softness – and the pain – but the hardness had melted. These were the eyes of a kind, loving man, the man she loved, with whom she wanted to spend the rest of her days.

Three weeks later Mary was discharged. It was a great homecoming with his mother at the door to welcome them. Inside the warm, comfortable kitchen the kettle was singing on the Rayburn and the smell of fresh apple tart with cinnamon reminded them both of the comforts of home. Just as they were about to sit down, Colm went over to the little crib where his son lay, lifted him gently and said,

'I think we'll call him Michael.' Then he went outside and walked directly to the gate that opened onto the field. He closed it behind him. As he did so the two women, watching from the kitchen window, saw him smile at the infant, cradle him in his arms. Then he sat down on the grassy mound under his tree.

'We'll give them some time together and then I'll make the tea,' said his mother, as she rinsed the hot water in the teapot and left it sitting on the edge of the cooker in preparation for her son and grandson's return.

Pancakes

When I see them on a menu I can never resist them. They're not just plain, simple pancakes anymore, but carry the grand title of 'Crepes Suzette' or they may be described as 'Stuffed Pancakes filled with Spinach and Mozzarella' or other combinations. There are all kinds nowadays, from savoury ones, filled with exotic spices to the dessert ones that make the mouth water. I make them often, just the plain ones for myself and for my grandchildren, and relish in the delight that they love them just as much as I did when I was a child. We are told that what happens to us in childhood affects us for the rest of our lives. Perhaps that's why an insatiable desire for pancakes has remained with me to the present time! It all goes back to one Shrove Tuesday. If I lived in the US I could ask my therapist to unravel the mysterious hold they have on me, but since I don't, I find it's much simpler to go on making and eating pancakes whenever I feel the urge.

In our house, as in every other house on our street, pancakes were made on Shrove Tuesday. It was the custom to celebrate with a feast of them before the Fast, because on Ash Wednesday the serious business of Fast and Abstinence began. It continued for all of forty days and was a miserable period for adults and children alike. We had to 'Give Up' for Lent, the subject of much discussion and direction from parents and teachers alike. We were not willing volunteers; sometimes suggesting to our audience that we hadn't yet decided what 'it' might be. When I finally came up with the idea of giving up Christmas cake I was told,

'You're giving up sweets and that's that!' I seldom held out for the forty days and fell several times on the way but each time I stole a sweet I felt great and then resolved to do better next time. Easter Sunday was a far-distant, dim ray of hope, with its promise of good things to come, but it offered little encouragement in those early days of Lent. And so, Shrove Tuesday or Pancake Tuesday, as we preferred to call it, was second only to Christmas and Hallowe'en. I would have given up turkey and pud any day for one of my mother's pancakes.

As a small child, I never knew what they were made of; I loved to think that they were magic. Somehow, the mixture appeared in the big glass jug; that lovely, rich, creamy, silky-pouring liquid, just waiting to flow onto the pan, at the command of the pourer. The black Stanley Range was waiting and ready. Good dry turf had been poked and raked at regular intervals and other small, dry sods tenderly added, one by one, so as not to upset the balance of heat. There were small pancakes and big ones, but all shared the same process, gradually mutating to send up those pock-like air holes, as the underside of the mixture cooked. Then came the exciting moment of the 'flip over', when we all had the privilege of watching the repeat performance onto a plate, held in readiness for the great moment! The pancake was ready to be eaten.

Some were eaten as soon as they were cooked, because my mother could no longer ignore the expectant, longing look on our faces, as we stood at the side of the range. Every so often, she gingerly opened the cast iron lid of the firebox, in order to add more turf. It was vital to keep the red-hot coals glowing, or the mixture on the pan would die a slow, anaemic death and become a pancake fit only for the cat.

The first pancake tasted best of all. The dollop of country butter was generously heaped into the middle and gradually slid down the sides, so that even when the pancake was eaten fingers could be sucked, until they were licked clean. The first ones cooked were ceremoniously doled out according to age (why it was done in reverse process I never knew and didn't dare ask, in case I risked losing out) but I, being the youngest, got mine first. It was about the only time that the age thing worked in my favour. Always the first to have to go to bed, always the one who had to wear the hand-me-downs, to do whatever I was told to do by the other siblings.

'Because you're the youngest and I said so!'

Anyway, back to the Pancake Tuesday when it all went wrong. I had been counting the days. On Monday I caught a bug, the wrong one, a vomiting bug. By Tuesday morning I felt much better and assured my mother I was fine. She wasn't convinced and announced that I needed to fast for another day. I was devastated and said that I would be fasting for forty days. She was having none of it. The only feast for me at tea, that fateful evening, was feasting my eyes on each and every one of my family members, as they downed the pancakes. The worst was to come, when my pancake was given to my brother, who gave me that look that only he and I understood. I sat in the big, old armchair, beside the range, usually occupied by my father. I just watched them all eat until my oldest brother swallowed the last morsel of the last pancake. Then he proceeded to lick each of his ten fingers with his eyes fixed on me. I was badly wounded! In the years that followed I enjoyed many Pancake Tuesdays, but I have never forgotten the year that, for me, Lent began on Pancake Tuesday and lasted for forty-one days!

The Tartan Slippers

If only she had been given the time to say goodbye. That summer, they had spent a lot of time together; lazy days in the sunshine, with walks in the woods behind the house and the coffee pot always on the stand.

'I'll have another cup of that brew,' he'd say. 'Great stuff for the thirst. Not as good as the pint but not all that bad.'

'You know you shouldn't. The doctor says it's bad for your heart. It sets it racing.'

'Sure what does he know? He's way overweight himself and he tells me what I should be doing, or rather not doing! I don't heed a thing he says. My heart is fine. His won't be half as good when he gets to my age. He's full of talk and only keeps blabbing on so that he can justify taking my hard-earned money. They're a shower of robbers, those boys.'

There was no point in arguing with him. He was a stubborn man who generally got his own way. A bit too fond of the jar, though he would never admit it. They seemed to be always fighting but loved each other to bits. Ever since his wife had died he had become more and more dependent on his only daughter, Sally, but he never allowed her to dictate to him.

She was in the hospital ward with him the first time he was admitted with chest pains. The list of questions went on and on. By the second day he had had enough. When another young doctor appeared in the doorway with his file, he became more and more annoyed. The questions were the same but this time the answers were different.

'Have you have regular bowel movements, Mr Hennessy?'

'Indeed, I do. They're moving all the time with loads of wind since last night. It's those damn tinned beans they gave me for tea yesterday. Tell them in the kitchen not to give me any more. I thought there was a chef here and I was sure I'd have the luxury of a nice bit of food. Sure, any wee lass can open a tin of beans.' He was in his element and enjoying every minute of his own performance, but even she was not prepared for what came next.

'Do you smoke?'

'Only cigarettes.'

'How many a day?'

'It all depends.'

What about drink, Sir?'

'Nice of you to offer but it's a bit early in the day. Have one yourself if you like!' Whether the list was complete or not the young man left the room in a hurry, without as much as a hint of a smile.

But that first time in hospital was the start of his illness and gradual decline. The trips to hospital became more frequent. Still, he held on, smoked his fag and drank his pint. She thought he'd go on forever and could never imagine things would change.

'I wonder if they do as good a job cleaning the pipes up there as they do down here,' he'd say.

'Where?' she'd ask.

'Up in Heaven or wherever we go. This is a clean, cool, creamy pint and my heaven. If I had the choice it's where I'd stay for eternity.' He'd never look at her, but, instead, he'd take that pint in his hand and savour the white froth that made him look like a bearded Santa.

She had stayed with him for four weeks after his last discharge and finally had packed her bags and returned to Dublin. She promised she would see him at the weekend.

'Come on Friday,' he called to her as she left. On Friday she rang to say it would be Saturday before she could come.

'You said you'd be down on Friday. I've two lovely steaks, with all the trimmings, in the fridge.'

'It has to be tomorrow, Dad.'

'I'll have to get into town to buy new shoes. My feet are tortured in these ones.'

'We'll have plenty of time on Saturday. Anyway, why can't you wear the lovely slippers, that I bought for you, around the house?'

'I'd look a right 'eejit' in those tartan yokes! I hate the look of them and the colour is all wrong.' It was as simple as that, contrary as ever!

'Know something, Dad? You're impossible.'

'You're the one who's impossible,' came the reply as he slammed down the phone.

As she pulled up at the house on Saturday she was surprised to see her neighbour come out the front door.

'I don't want to alarm you but your Dad collapsed and has been taken to hospital by ambulance. I'll go with you straight away after you've had a cup of tea. I didn't want to ring your mobile when you were driving. He was able to tell me you'd be here before three.'

She feared the worst but was not prepared for the shock she got when she entered the room. This was different! Only the shell of the big man remained. He seemed to be drained of everything that had given energy to his body. Her whole body began to tremble and she could do nothing to stop it. Suddenly, she felt afraid. His face was ashen grey; so unlike his usual colour. No sign of recognition in the eyes that appeared to be fixed on the light bulb overhead. Not one word from him. It was like looking at a stranger. She turned to the nurse, hoping for some words of encouragement, but she only shook her head and fumbled with his chart at the foot of the bed.

She sat down beside him and took his hand in hers. It remained limp and felt icy cold. How she longed to hear that voice call out to her and scold her, as he had so often done, saying too much or too little milk was making his tea too hot or too cold! This could not be happening. Did he know what was going on or did he feel any pain?

Evening turned into night but this was not the normal weekend night to which she had been looking forward. The fire by now getting low and her father slowly getting up from his rocking chair to build it up again with turf. On the stroke of eleven he'd put two glasses on the table, take out the brandy and announce to her

'Have a little drop! It'll help you sleep. Sure, I might as well join you and keep you company. It would be a shame to see you having a drink on your own.' Then he'd reminisce:

'Do you mind the day we went to Dublin to the Zoo?'

How could she ever forget... candy floss, which she had never even seen before, chicken and chips, ice cream and a whole day full of excitement, while he pointed out all the animals. They had both enjoyed every moment of the trip. He gave out for days about the price of the entrance fee, but she knew that he had enjoyed it as much as she had. Then there was the day that she had fallen off her bike and broken the lamp.

'It's not very sensible to be running into walls, you know. Didn't I often tell you not to be going so fast?' he said, as he dried her tears and cleaned her sore knee. Next day, there was a brand new lamp on her bike but he had always claimed that he hadn't put it there.

She must have dozed a little, because suddenly it was dawn. Looking out she saw the first rays of sunlight on the damp hedges and on the grass below, while the early daffodils sparkled as they bore the remnants of raindrops on their tips. He loved daffodils and suddenly she felt her throat tighten, as she tried to fight the tears swelling up within her. Meanwhile the figure in the bed had not stirred and the room seemed stifling after the long night, as the nurses made their rounds. They spoke kindly to her but could tell her nothing. He was stable but critical. She should go and have some breakfast downstairs. She agreed.

Suddenly her mobile rang.

'He's asking for you but you need to come at once.' The lift took ages. People were getting in and out at every floor. She wanted to scream at them but couldn't find her voice. Anger swelled up within her while her throat went dry. Why couldn't they all stay where they were until she had reached the sixth floor? A young mother, with one small child in a buggy, and two older children by her side, was trying to negotiate the lift, while a well-meaning gentleman held the doors open. She could stand it no longer and almost knocked one of the youngsters over as she rushed out. She climbed the last two flights, taking the steps two at a time. Hospital staff, relieved to have finished the night shift, chatted to each other as they passed. She felt a pang of jealousy that the day for them was just the same as any other. Life in the hospital would go on as usual, death being part of that normality - that is for those on the fringes. Only the main actors, the subjects of the drama were the focus. As in a wilderness, she felt totally lost and isolated. Never had she felt so alone, on her own.

She knew it was all over when she saw the nurse's face.

'His heart stopped just after we called you. He is at peace. He regained consciousness for a few moments and called your name, but the effort exhausted him and he just closed his eyes and passed away.'

'I wish...' but the words choked her. If only she hadn't gone downstairs for breakfast. One breakfast out of all the thousands she would have! If only she had come home yesterday. How could she live with those 'Ifs' for the rest of her days! She wondered if the dull pain she now felt would ease with time. She was a child in need of someone to comfort her. She longed to hear his voice scolding her.

'You'll have to help me through this,' she sobbed to the silent figure of her father in the bed.

The following days passed as though she were in a dream. Removal, funeral, crowds in the house with the usual 'Sorry for your trouble,' which seemed to be the only comment ringing in her ears. He would be no trouble to her now, sure he never was! He would no longer be a part of her life.

Bit by bit the neighbours and friends, whose own lives had been put on 'Pause', returned to their homes and normality. Only Olive, her immediate neighbour, stayed behind. The noise and chatter of the previous days gave way to an unbearable silence.

There was plenty to talk about, but they only spoke in whispers, as they sipped more tea.

Finally, Sally mounted the stairs to the bedroom as Olive followed behind. There, beside the bed, were the pair of tartan slippers, each with a sock stuffed inside. She felt a great sadness as she looked at them. For a few moments they both remained silent. Then, in a quiet voice, Olive said

'He told me he was wearing them just to please you but confided in me that he did think they were rather cute! Would you like a few minutes on your own?'

'No, Olive. I don't want to be on my own just now. But I suppose I'll have to try to get on with things. There is so much to do and I know you'll always be there for me. You've been a great friend ever since mum died. I know my dad thought so too, even though he mightn't have often told you so!' She hugged the old family friend and suddenly they both started laughing.

'That's more like it.'

Sally walked the older woman to the door and as she turned to go inside the full moon shone on the stained-glass window in the hall and threw its light along the corridor, as she made her way upstairs. She had already decided not to go back to work for a while. She wondered what she should do about the house. Maybe she'd sell it and make the apartment in Dublin her permanent home.

At the top of the stairs she turned again into her father's room and opened the drawer of his bedside locker. In it were all the postcards from her holidays abroad, held together with rubber bands. He had penned in the dates on every one of them. Photographs were in the second drawer, the one at the Zoo on top. As she took them out to browse through them, a small key, with her name on it, fell to the ground. It was the key to the little drawer in the dressing table where he kept his important papers. She opened it and saw an envelope with 'For You Sally' written on it. In it were two sheets of paper. The first carried a list of all his important documents and the numbers of Bank Accounts etc. She turned to the second folded sheet of paper and began to read.

'Sally, I've known since that first visit to hospital that my time is almost up. Last week I had a check-up and my condition has deteriorated further. I forbade them to tell you. There is nothing more that can be done. I am a man who has lived life to the full and when my time comes I want to die with the harness on my back! You and I have had great times together. I want to enjoy life up to the very last moment. I would like you to hold onto the house and to come home at week-ends. It will keep you in touch with your roots and I think it would be good for you. Do one other thing for me, please! On Saturday nights take out the brandy and pour a glass for each of us. I'll be with you in spirit!'

The Photograph

It's getting late and I have not found that document that I misplaced. I need it tomorrow morning. I decide to have another look through the drawers of the old cabinet in the corner of the kitchen. It is an unlikely place, but I may have absentmindely put it there. Nothing in the first two drawers so I pull at the bottom one, which is generally hard to open. Using as much force as possible I tug it open. An old album drops to the floor and a faded photograph falls out. I pick it up and suddenly the urgency of my search is forgotten as my mind wanders to times past.

I was about seven years of age when this picture was taken. I have no idea who took it, but I recognise the childhood friends as if it were yesterday. I look at my sister with a great sadness that has never lifted in all the years that have passed. She was too young to die. She is so full of life, looking directly at the camera. I remember that smile so well. It is a denial of the reality that she would be cut off so young. I feel I can almost touch her, see her flip back her hair as she spoke. It was jet black, tied in a red ribbon. Her eyes are big and solemn, yet full of fun. The photo is in black and white but the colours are clear in my mind's eye.

How well I remember the tweed coat with the brown trimming that I am wearing! It was a hand-me-down from her. All my clothes were hers until I grew taller, even though I was younger. I like to place the time in May, a Saturday morning perhaps, when we all played together in the old castle grounds, beside the stream. May was always her favourite month. We're sitting on the grass, all smiling happily, waiting for those long summer holidays not too far away. Who among us had a camera, I wonder? I can't think who it might have been. She is the one who gave us that moment, now history, but her own story is silent.

I can still hear the song of the stream, babbling over the stones, as it wound its way to I don't know where. We paddle and select our stones with great care and play a game of moving large ones so that we can change the direction of the flow of water. Nothing to interrupt us and we have all day. The sandwiches have been put in a safe place between two large boulders on the grass verge and are not to be eaten yet. One of us checks from time to time just to make sure that they are still there. Changing the flow of the stream was a serious business and we had to work hard. What matter if all our efforts were in vain and the stream reverted to its natural course! Our stones would still be there for all to see. Later in life we would learn that the direction of our lives would follow its own course too. For now we were carefree with nothing to mar our joy.

Memories, even those tinged with sadness, are precious. I have spent a long time looking at this one photo, finally moving on to others that I haven't seen for years. The album is old, its pages a portrait of other days. Night has fallen, the fire needs rekindling, and I still have to find that document. I get up to fetch some logs and throw them into the firebox. Soon it will be time for bed. For now, I will watch the late night news with all its urgency of the present and the future, which, in turn, will also become a memory.

A Christmas Story

They sat side by side in front of the Stanley Range, watching the glow of the red hot embers. Neither spoke, lost in their thoughts. The younger girl occasionally glanced at her older sister as if for reassurance. Everything was so lovely tonight; the warmth of the fire giving a feeling of peace. She could imagine all kinds of wonderful scenes as she gazed at the hot coals piled against the rungs of the open firebox. She was the princess and her prince charming was right there in front of the massive lump of coal, which, of course, had now become his castle. He would come for her one day and never leave her. Again she looked at her older sister who called her a 'Silly Billy' when she heard her playing her games out loud. She was so wise and good. Mama never had to scold her and she always talked to her about grown-up things. She wondered when she would be grown-up enough to share such conversations with her mother.

But tonight everything was perfect, or almost perfect. It was Christmas Eve and the silence was laden with expectation. It was just the same as last year, and every other year as far back as she could remember. When they were washed and ready for bed the nicest thing happened. They were allowed to stay up late, sitting at the fire, looking for signs of Santa. Even as she looked now she was sure she saw him smiling at her. That would be her secret!

She looked at her mother and just at that moment their eyes met. She wanted to tell her that she loved her and that she was going to be very good from now on. Mama got so upset at times and it always ended in tears. The day she had broken that big vase in the hall her mother had been very cross and told her that she could never replace it. She had made her a 'Sorry' card next day, but Mama seemed to get even more upset when she gave it to her. Adults were very complicated!

Her mother, too, was deep in her own thoughts. She cherished this moment; the silence and peace of Christmas all around! She knew she was fortunate to have her two beautiful little girls, who were healthy and happy, though Amy could be quite a handful at times. She would have to try to be more patient with her – she was such a little baby in every way and looked so like her Dad. If only this moment would last forever. When the Carol Singers had called to the door earlier she felt the tears come as they sang 'Silent Night, Holy Night.' It was just the same as last year and every other year. For just one moment she had forgotten. During these few days she would not allow any worries to spoil the celebration of Christmas. The turkey was ready in the pantry, and tomorrow they would all enjoy opening their presents in the sitting room upstairs. These were the only few days in the year that the turf was carried up and the fire lit. She hoped there wouldn't be a blowdown. It all depended on the direction of the wind.

Amy looked at her mother again. She was so beautiful that she wanted to hug her, but she was afraid that if she moved the spell would be broken and the moment spoiled. If only tonight could go on forever! She wondered why her mother often looked sad, but just now she was smiling. She didn't dare tell her that she was so afraid of everything, even of Santa Claus. Most of all she was afraid that she was never going to see her father again. But tonight, she was happy. Mama, Breege and she had something very special.

Earlier in the evening the singers had come to their door, collecting for poor people. They had sung 'Silent Night' so beautifully. The words 'Silent' and 'Holy' were special. Tomorrow was Christmas Day and Granny and Uncle Jim would arrive for dinner. There would be a lot of noise and laughter, but she preferred the silence they now shared. Would Mama let her set the table on her own? She was five and a half years old now and well able to do it. But Breege always bossed her around the place. Sometimes she really hated her. It was all right to be mad with her at times because the teacher had told them that you must love your neighbour and Breege was her sister, not her neighbour. Last year when she had helped to set the table, she knew she had done a good job putting everything in place, with folded napkins sitting beautifully on the forks. Breege had looked at the table and said

'Don't you know how to count, Amy? There are only five of us.' She had made no reply but Mama had seen the tears in her eyes.

'Leave her alone, Breege. It's all right, Amy! You've done a great job.'

The embers began to fade and still Mama did not ask them to go to bed. She became sleepy and comfortable and snuggled closer to her sister. Maybe she wasn't so bad after all! She began to think about her letter to Santa. She prayed hard that he would have read it in time to bring her the only thing she wanted. She stared and stared at the fire and then had a great idea. She hadn't thought of it before even though when Teacher had told them about the 'Neighbour' thing she had also told them about the Angel whose job it was to mind each one of them. Why hadn't she thought of it?

'Please, please, Angels in Heaven, give us back our Dada for Christmas,' she whispered. She waited for an answer but all she heard was

'Off to bed with you girls now or Santa wont come.' The two little ones scampered up the stairs and into bed. As Amy snuggled down into her blankets she wondered what the morning would bring!

A Cat and A Car

Life was simple in the small town and its clock moved slowly. Anything out of the ordinary was always a welcome diversion and Miss Mc Creedy's new car, sitting outside her front door on a Saturday morning, caused quite a stir. How it came to be parked there without anyone seeing it was the topic of conversation. She couldn't drive! The old high bike she had cycled for years was so much a part of her that, somehow, the idea of her owning a car did not fit in.

But Miss Mc Creedy was determined to move with the times! Very few people owned cars in the 1950's and those that did were generally well off. Rumours began to circulate, a bit of money from an old aunt in the States perhaps! Unaware of the gossip, Miss Mc Creedy got down to the business of taking to the road with varying degrees of success and a rather nervous disposition. Somehow it wasn't as easy as riding a bike. Progress was slow.

She took to blowing the horn at every opportunity and was easily recognized by the two beeps in quick succession, as she drove up the street. Sunday Mass wasn't attempted until she felt a little more confident and had more practice at parking. Even then she had to get to the church at an unearthly hour. That way she had the whole road to herself and could park along the footpath without an audience. She had to remain in the church, on the pretext of praying, until she felt sure everyone else was gone. Starting off in first gear posed a lot of problems and when she finally shot off like a bird, with a screech of clutch and a roar of the engine, she left behind a billow of smoke.

That wasn't all. Negotiating corners gave her headaches! At one dangerous bend she lost her nerve and got out to see if anything was coming towards her. There wasn't. The unfortunate thing was that the local doctor, coming from behind at the critical moment, had to swerve violently at the last minute, taking the right-hand orange indicator with him as he went. She had difficulty with those indicators from the start, putting out the right to turn right, but then deciding at the last minute to turn left. She had a strict policy of never passing anything or anybody and even the postman on his 'High Nelly' often overtook her when on his rounds. Truth to tell, she missed the little chats she used to have with him, when she could easily hop down from her bike to have a word.

The donkeys and carts en route to the creamery, with their milk cans rattling as they trundled along, were the signal for her to stay indoors until she felt sure that they were well out of the way. But nothing is set in stone! She did get caught one morning a few miles out of town behind a cart, whose owner was enjoying a pull of plug tobacco as he released the reins on the donkey. She resigned herself to a lengthy, slower than usual, trip into town. The man, unaware of her predicament, slowed up to light his pipe and stopped several times to let other carts join the queue, holding his place in front of the Morris Minor! By the time they all got into town there were a number of carts in front, the Morris Minor in the middle and a couple of other carts bringing up the rear.

She had a lot of bother getting used to the various switches on the dashboard. One day she decided to visit her cousin, announcing that she wouldn't be staying late, because she hated night driving. The real reason was that she had taped over the headlight switches.

There was enough to contend with without complicating matters! She went through the format of starting off, pulled out the choke, hung her small handbag on it and off she went! The journey to Ellie's was delightful and it went without a hitch; it was on the return trip that she got a strong smell of something, she couldn't say exactly what, but a short distance from her cousin's house she heard a bit of a splutter and the car came to a slow but definite stop. Nothing for it but to get out and walk back the short distance to announce

'I will be staying the night after all.'

That was the first of many visits to the local garage! Miss Mc Creedy was quite happy with her progress, despite what she described as 'minor hiccups'. The wits in the pub referred to these upsets as 'Minor Hiccups' and that radical surgery (for the car!) was required on the day she had accelerated into the back of a parked van. She got a shock when she realised she was driving too close to the footpath and only noticed the van at the very last moment. In her confusion, she accelerated, instead of applying the brakes.

'I always need time to concentrate and ask myself "Is it the right pedal or the left pedal that I use now?" That's all that happened.'

Bit by bit, the car lost its shiny, new look and all the bumps and scratches took their toll. It became more obvious, as time went on, that she, the car and the mechanic, her right-hand man, were wearing down little by little. She couldn't get the hang of reversing and he refused to tell her how, adding that he would not be responsible for her killing herself or anyone else.

The final straw was the death of Tabby. Tabby was Miss Mc Creedy's faithful and only companion, who, it was rumoured, slept with her. It was a lovely morning in early summer and Tabby had already taken up her favourite spot on the bonnet of the car. She was sleeping quietly, rolled up into a ball, motionless. Afterwards, it was argued, that because she was black, like the car, Miss Mc Creedy never noticed her. Others claimed that her eyesight had been failing for some time and that when Tom Groarty's dog had been knocked down some weeks previously, the only person on the road that day, between ten and eleven o'clock, had been Miss Mc Creedy. She was totally oblivious of all the speculation and gossip and when she met Tom's wife in the grocery shop she sympathised most sincerely on the death of the dog. Mrs Groarty hadn't the heart to tell her that she was the prime suspect.

Miss Mc Creedy had gained in confidence, if not in execution, and the bright sky and early sunshine had her in a happy frame of mind. With eyes and left hand firmly on the gearshift she shot into reverse for the first time ever and the car flew back in jumps. Taking a moment to recover, she changed into first gear and moved slowly away from the footpath. She was really getting the hang of it at last. That was the fatal moment! Tabby had been thrown from the bonnet under the right front wheel, a bit stunned but unharmed, until the poor little thing was crushed as the car moved forward. Its owner drove away, unaware of the tragedy, until her return an hour later when the cat had already passed on to wherever cats go.

'I should have been there for her,' she sobbed.

'What happened?'

All remained silent until finally Paddy Mc said cautiously,

'I think she got under the wheel of your car.'

Miss Mc Creedy went into her house and remained there for

the rest of the week. The only person to whom she opened the door was the mechanic. That was a Sunday. She hadn't even been seen at either of the Masses, although Mary Bee swore she had walked to the church late Saturday night. Everyone knew you couldn't believe the Lord's Prayer from her so that theory was dismissed without further discussion.

As quietly as it had appeared, the Morris Minor disappeared. On Monday morning it was nowhere to be seen. Even when Mary Bee went into the garage, to get a leak in an old saucepan soldered, the car was nowhere to be seen.

'The car's gone.'

'Is that so?' came the reply, the only reply the mechanic gave to all who enquired after Miss Mc Creedy's health. A few days later, the squeaking of an old bike could be heard on Main Street, and a smiling Miss Mc Creedy appeared, pedalling slowly as always.

Two of a Kind?

It began with a double wedding. Money was scarce and the two brothers had none to spare. Neither had the two brides-to-be. Hugh and Tony were hard workers, but the land was wet and heavy and only suitable for grass and milch cows. Hugh had fallen in for the bachelor uncle's farm of thirty acres, which gave each of them his own bit of ground and independence. While the main income for each house would come from cows' milk they still continued to work together, making hay, lifting the spuds and saving the turf.

Ellen was very excited at the prospect of a double wedding. Nora was less impressed. A quiet girl, who had never left home, she was somewhat in awe of Ellen, who had worked in Mahon's Drapery from the time she had left school at fourteen. It came naturally to her to set about making the arrangements and twenty per cent discount on the dress material was most welcome. At first Nora had been pleased that Ellen was organising everything, but then she realised that she was only consulted when decisions had already been made.

'I would love a bouquet of sweet pea,' she said, as the two of them sat on the wall outside her future home.

'They're nice in a vase and have a lovely scent but they would never last the day,' replied Ellen. 'I've already asked my Aunt Mary for some of the beautiful roses from her garden. She has even promised to make up a hand posy for each of us. I'll have the red and she'll do up the cream ones for you.'

'I really like sweet pea,' Nora said timidly, but Ellen had caught sight of Hugh coming out of the cow byre and called out to him as she hopped down from the wall.

'What's keeping Tony?'

'He'll be here shortly. I started milking before him.' He joined the two girls as Ellen babbled on about Mrs Cooney asking how the wedding plans were coming on.

'You're very quiet this evening, Nora,' Hugh remarked.

'I'm just a bit tired, that's all.'

Two months later the couples married. It was a glorious day in June, one to remember. The brides were beautiful and the two brothers, in their new suits, looked very handsome. Ellen carried a posy of red roses and Nora a similar one in cream. They went to Dublin for the weekend, staying in a guest house in North Circular Rd, near the Cattle Market. All too soon it was time to go home to settle down to their new life. Ellen would continue to work a few days a week in Mahon's while Nora set about decorating the uncle's house. She enjoyed cycling into town to choose the wallpaper and paint. Hugh was very handy and was often called on to do odd jobs for the neighbours. Any extra cash would go towards making the house more comfortable. Nora was a very good seamstress, as was her mother before her, and the hand 'Singer' sewing machine had moved with her. When the first flour bag was finally empty, it was washed, bleached and embroidered with a perfect chain stitch, to form the letter H. It would not be long before the next flour bag would have Nora's initial on the corner and then would come the tea towels, sheets and embroidered tray cloths. Bright cushions helped to cover the dip in the old armchairs and Hugh sanded down the wooden arm rests and stained them with a few coats of varnish till they shone like new. The only one to complain about the dip in the middle was Ellen!

'Hugh, can't you get me a decent chair to sit on? My back is breaking on this thing. Bring me the straight backed one from the parlour, please.' She and her husband had the habit of dropping in every night. Nora had begun to get tired of it but she said nothing. The two brothers took it for granted that they were now a foursome. The occasional outing to the cinema, or to the parish hall, to enjoy the local drama group's play, became the norm. Sometimes Nora would have liked to go somewhere, anywhere, with Hugh only but she was too shy to suggest it, and she did not want to hurt her husband's feelings. She loved the days on the bog, especially when Ellen was at work, when she chatted easily with the two brothers. She took great pride in feeding them well too. In the morning she got up early to bake her soda cake. When it had cooled on the window outside the kitchen she cut it, smothered it in homemade butter, before spreading thick slices of cold salted bacon on it to make the finest sandwiches ever eaten. She was a good cook and made delicious apple cakes every weekend. She had found the old cookery book that had belonged to her mother, entitled 'Full and Plenty' by Maura Laverty. Hugh loved her cooking and Tony often joined them for an evening meal, while Ellen was still at work.

One evening Ellen arrived with an armchair she had 'picked up' at the second-hand shop. Nora was really touched by her kindness. That was until she demanded the fifteen shillings she had paid for it!

'At last a chair I can sit in!' The colour was all wrong, a horrible shade of yellow, but Nora figured she could dress it up with odd pieces from her sewing bag. Hugh seemed a bit taken back and when he handed over the money he simply said,

'Next time you see a bargain, let us know first and we'll decide whether we want it or not.' Ellen just tossed her head and replied

'Sure you'd never buy a thing if I wasn't around to help.' Nora knew that this was true and was really fond of Ellen, even if she could be very tiresome and even interfering. One evening in early August she announced,

'I'll come over in the morning to give you a hand making the sandwiches for the haymaking in the far meadow. It's my first time this year and I feel I'm missing out. Tony keeps talking about all the fun you three have together.'

True to her word she arrived just as Nora was cutting the soda cake. She chattered away as she put plenty of butter on the bread, but although Nora had handed her a plate full of lovely slices of bacon, she seemed more intent on sparing the meat and spreading loads of 'Colman's Mustard' on every slice.

'I've plenty of bacon if you're short,' Nora volunteered.

'There's enough on them,' came the short reply. 'We'll leave some for a bite to eat when we all come home for dinner.'

Nora said nothing, but she had already detected a note of jealousy in Ellen's voice. They worked hard all morning and time flew. When they stopped for lunch, Hugh was the first to take a big bite from his sandwich. He stopped, with his mouth full and asked,

'Who made the mustard sandwiches?' The two women laughed but Hugh didn't, and Nora vowed that it would never happen again. She'd just have to learn to be less intimidated by Ellen. That night, after the couple had finally gone home, Nora told Hugh that she was pregnant.

'Don't say anything to the others yet. There'll be plenty of time.'

When she was in the fourth month of her pregnancy, she broke the news to Ellen and Tony. She saw Ellen glance quickly at Tony before she spoke.

'I'm expecting too,' she announced. The months passed and Ellen was first to give birth to a baby boy. A month later Nora also gave birth to a baby boy. Hugh and she had agreed on a name long before she was due; if it was a girl she would name her after her mother and if it was a boy he would be given Hugh's father's name, Patrick. As usual, Ellen got there first.

'He'll be christened Patrick John after our two fathers but he'll be called Patrick.' Nora didn't mind but she knew that Hugh was disappointed. He had to be happy with Joseph Patrick. Both mothers were kept busy with their newborn sons and, for the first few months, saw very little of each other. It was when Ellen decided to go back to work that Nora readily agreed to mind Patrick for the three days each week. The two babies were quite a handful, but she was not afraid of work and it was nice for the cousins to be together. They were good babies and as their first birthdays came near Nora found it hard to believe that a whole year had passed. Soon it was their second birthdays and here were two little boys who played and laughed together all day long. They were different in temperament; Patrick was very outgoing and liked to order his cousin around, while Joseph was shy and less adventurous.

Then came the day when they both started school and neighbours' children collected them. They would soon be able to go on their own, but for the moment it was nice to see the older ones looking out for them. Joseph was first to be collected and a short distance away Patrick waited with his mother on the street outside their house. They could hear the noisy chatter as the children came nearer. Patrick could not wait; he let go of his mother's hand as soon as he caught sight of Joseph, who was looking rather weepy and trying to hold back his tears.

The two children soon settled into school and looked up to the big boys and girls in The Master's Room. Time came when they were big boys themselves and on their way to the local secondary school. They were firm friends by then, more like brothers than cousins. Ellen had three more children and Nora had another baby, a little girl. The two men continued to farm; the price for milk was good and they worked hard to provide for their families. The women were kept busy with the household chores and the foursome outings were rare. Ellen had given up her job with the arrival of her second child, but she was not partial to housework and became very restless and cantankerous. She missed the shop and her friends, for she was a 'townie' at heart. Nora watched her change and was relieved when Patrick and Joseph were put into different classes in their second year.

'Patrick is in the top class,' she announced when Nora called.

'I wonder why Joseph didn't get in too.' Without waiting for an answer she went on,

'He's easy learned and he has twelve hard-backed books in his new class. How many has Joseph?' Nora ignored the slight on her son but kept her cool. From then on Ellen appeared to be obsessed with her son's education and could speak of nothing else. Meanwhile, the two boys were unaware of the tension between the mothers, while their fathers did their best to ignore it but even they were becoming uneasy. Test results were compared and when Patrick got the highest mark in his class for an essay, Ellen could talk of nothing else. Joseph wasn't in the least upset by the news! Patrick was embarrassed and the boys quietly agreed among themselves that from then on they would get the same marks, more or less. Sometimes Joseph was a mark or two higher, sometimes lower. It was a simple matter to alter the marks; a nought was an eight, a three a five and so on. They enjoyed themselves. There was no harm in keeping Patrick's mother happy and it worked for a while.

But Ellen was not at all happy. She wanted great things for her first-born. He was not going to spend his life on a small farm if she had anything to do with it. He could then help the younger children along. One morning in late January Nora called to the house. The kitchen was a mess, ashes flying everywhere, as Ellen absentmindedly raked the coals in the open hearth.

'I'd love our Patrick to be a doctor but he'll have to study harder,' she announced to no-one in particular, as she sat back on her heels and blew more ashes up on the mantel in an attempt to get the fire going. From then on, Patrick had to go to his room and start his homework earlier. He did not object; he had his own way of dealing with his mother. He could slip out the back window, through the hedge and make his way to the field behind the barn where he kicked a ball. He was always back in his room before his mother was due to call him down for a cup of tea. Tony was no match for Ellen; she was the boss and that was that. He smoked his pipe and drank the odd pint when he and his brother went to play darts in the local pub.

Joseph never worried about schoolwork. He was a happy youngster who liked nothing better than to join his father and give a helping hand as soon as he came home from school. Neither his father nor his mother knew much about education and Joseph was largely left to his own devices. Theirs was a happy house. Still, his marks were good and he had built up a sound relationship with his parents. He chatted easily to them about his friends and they enjoyed listening to the stories he told of events in school.

On a Sunday afternoon in early March, Nora and Hugh decided to call on the others. Their timing was wrong; they stopped dead in their tracks as the sound of loud voices could be clearly heard coming from the kitchen. They were about to turn around and leave, when the back door opened and Tony came out, looking very upset. Ellen continued to shout, unaware of the callers.

'Herself is losing it,' and he pulled out his pipe and sucked on its emptiness.

'I think it'd be better if I went down to your place till she calms down. All this talk about being a doctor! It's not what the lad wants and I tried to tell her. She doesn't listen to me. I don't know her anymore. This education business has gone to her head. True as God if it isn't raining the wind is on the door.' He attempted a smile and pulled once more on his empty pipe.

The months passed and Nora never knew if Ellen was aware that they had called. Nothing more was said and it was several weeks before it was mentioned again. Tony and Hugh were cutting the turf, just the two of them, when Tony paused, one foot on the slean, ready to slice through the wet turf, when he looked up and said,

'It's all sorted. There'll be no more talk of what Patrick should do. I laid it firmly on the line and the matter is closed. I should have stood up to her a long time ago. It fair took the coal out of her pipe when I told her she'd drive the lad away. We're all getting on grand together now. We have to think of the other children as well.'

Still, when the two women were alone, Ellen never missed an opportunity to boast about Patrick.

'He's doing Honours Maths. Only four in his class are good enough.' Nora knew nothing of Honours Maths and she doubted if Ellen did either. At tea that evening she told Hugh about Ellen.

'I had a visit from "Honours Maths" today,' she said and from then on the two of them shared the joke and referred to Ellen by her new title, but never in the presence of their two children.

The Leaving Cert came and went and both boys were pleased with their results. Padraig (as his father now liked to call him) did well and Joseph, too, had done himself proud. He wanted to be a 'Garda' and sat the exam. So did Patrick and he was first to be called for interview. Ellen, of course, could not resist the opportunity to state to Nora, (when the men were down the fields) that it was obvious that Patrick's marks were higher than Joseph's; that was why he had been called first. Nora never pretended to notice the nasty remark. Joseph would be called, she felt and so he was.

It was at 'The Station Mass', five years later, that one of the neighbours from up the 'Big Brae' asked about the boys.

'I saw them both at Christmas, fine lads they are, and great friends as always. It's lovely that they're both in Dublin. I'm sure they spend a lot of time together,' Nora stirred herself. She had waited a long time. This was her chance.

'They're the best of friends,' she said 'but they don't see each other as often as they'd like. Joseph has been transferred to a different Station since he was promoted to Sergeant. You see, Patrick is still just a plain guard!'

Four stories at Christmas for our six Grandchildren

Stories to share with children all over the country
(and the child in all of us!)

Twinkle, the Little Star

The sky was bright blue, even though it was night. The little stars shone better than ever before and the grown-ups smiled proudly at each other. Their little ones were really doing a splendid job! Never before had a Christmas Eve been so bright. 'The Man In The Moon' beamed at them all. They were such a jolly bunch, a great team and he was delighted to share in their wonderful display on this special night.

But all was not well. Twinkle was so unhappy and so restless. He thought that if he took a trip down to Earth he might feel better. He wanted a bit of excitement in his life and could not be convinced that falling to earth was a dangerous game. His mother tried to talk him out of it.

'You are needed here. What would we do without you?' But Twinkle wasn't listening. He was in one of his moods again. What his mother hadn't told him was that one of his brother stars had gone tumbling to Earth in the previous century and had just burned up. She was very worried that Twinkle might do something foolish.

He hadn't been himself for some time now. What could it be? To tell the truth all that was wrong with Twinkle was that he was lonely. He had no real friends. The older stars were big enough to have races across the sky in the dead of night but he could never keep up. He was a bit ashamed too that his light was dimmer than all the others. His mother kept telling him that all he needed was a bit of confidence. Even so, he felt he would never be any good. On cloudy nights, when the stars could rest he would go into a corner of the sky and watch his brothers and sisters having great fun. He was a very shy star, and by the time he had plucked up the courage to join them, his mother always told him it was time for him to have a good sleep, so that he would grow up to be a fine, strong star.

Tonight, on Christmas Eve, he felt really sad. Unnoticed by the others, he shed a few tears, so that his light almost went out. Suddenly he sat right up and listened. What was it? Someone was calling his name. Not just that, someone called Jack and his little brother, Josh, were singing a lovely song all about him.

'Twinkle, Twinkle, little star,
How I wonder what you are?'

He couldn't believe what he was hearing and all the other stars had heard the singing too. They just couldn't believe it. Two lovely little boys had picked Twinkle out from all the rest and were singing to him. He raised his light to its full beam and shone as he has never shone before. There were 'Oohs and Ahs' from the others as they crowded round.

'You must be a very special star to have had a song written about you. I am so proud of you,' his mother said. Twinkle gave off twice as much light, as he smiled broadly at them all.

'I must really do a good job now,' he replied. 'My two earth friends are depending on me', and his light seemed to revolve even more, sending twinkly rays all over the sky, until his light was the brightest by far.

From their bedroom window two little boys gazed in wonder at the beauty of it all. They had never before seen anything so wonderful. Over and over they sang and when they came to the word 'diamond' they gasped as the star really did a twirl, showing them a glistening diamond in the frosty sky. Then the most extraordinary thing happened. It was as if Twinkle seemed to know that Jack and Josh had cousins who were all still up and awake and looking at the sky. First, there was Aoife down in Kerry and she had just gone into her bedroom to lower the blind. She said,

'Wow. Just look at that'. She took out her tin whistle and began to play 'Twinkle, Twinkle'. The star could hear the melodious strains and did dives and twirls that were amazing.

Up in Dublin were three more cousins and they were having great fun jumping on their parents' bed. They were supposed to be in their own rooms, but tonight was special and Mum and Dad were talking to some friends who had called. They wouldn't be disturbed for another while so why not have fun? Neil was beside the window and when he looked out he saw the most beautiful sight, a real star dancing in the sky.

'Look! Anna and Louise. Look at the star', and at once he and Anna began to sing

'Twinkle, Twinkle, Little Star
How I Wonder What You Are'.

Louise wasn't too sure of the words so she waited until the other two had finished and then she recited a little poem, all on her own, for Twinkle.

'Two little monkeys jumping on the bed
One fell off and hurt his head
Mama called for the doctor and the doctor said
No more monkeys jumping on the bed.'

Twinkle was overjoyed with all the attention. He skipped and dived and jumped as he never knew he could and all the children were still singing his song. Even Louise was getting the hang of it. It was the best night ever.

It had all begun when Jack and Josh had been so kind as to sing the 'Twinkle' song and now the whole sky was vibrating with the lovely sound of music, floating up from the earth below. The other stars were singing too and Twinkle thought he was going to burst with happiness.

As they finally snuggled down into their warm beds, Jack told his Mama that the little star had heard them singing and had turned up his light for them to see.

'We will sing every night before we go to bed,' he said. 'I think we made Twinkle very happy tonight.'

In fact, the little star, too, had made the other children happy, Aoife in Kerry and Neil, Anna and Louise in Dublin. When Anna got into her bed she laid her little wand, with a star on top, beside her to remind her of Twinkle. The beautiful star had made children all over the world happy, as he showed them his wondrous light. Twinkle would never, ever, be lonely again.

Granddad's Slippers

'Bring me my slippers, Jack. My feet are killing me,' said Granddad. It was Christmas Eve and the preparations for Christmas were almost finished. Jack and Josh had helped Granddad with the tree and now they just could not believe their eyes. It looked so beautiful that they kept running in and out of the sitting room every few minutes to have another look. All the decorations had taken a long time to put up; now they looked so nice. The coloured lights shone like rainbows in the sky; reds, purples, blues, pinks and greens. They all mingled to form so many other colours that they boys were certain had never been seen before. Jack had climbed carefully to the top of the tree to place the lovely white Santa on the very top. Josh was the one who turned the lights on and for once the boys were silent for a few minutes as they looked at the tree. They were so happy. Now and then one of them would decide to change something. Maybe the small Santa would look better on a different branch and Josh thought they should move the red robin up higher, because he wanted to be sure it could be seen. Santa would be most impressed. Then, when they had everything just perfect, they had a lovely supper in front of the fire and finally they began to feel sleepy.

'Now it's time for bed,' said Mum. 'Santa will be coming soon.' They put sweets and biscuits and a lovely ham sandwich on the table so that Santa would not go hungry. He had such a lot of work to do on Christmas Eve.

Up the stairs the two boys plodded, excitement making their toes tingle. After washing and saying their prayers they finally settled down in their nice cosy beds, wondering what toys Santa would bring. Soon they feel sound asleep.

It was a heavy thud that awoke Jack. He jumped up and rubbed his eyes. He was sure that Josh had fallen out of his bed again. He was always doing it! But not this time. He was fast asleep, lying on his back with a smile on his face. Jack wondered if he was dreaming. Maybe his dream was about Baby Jesus and the stable at Bethlehem, where the story of Christmas all began.

Suddenly, a terrible thought struck him. Maybe the Christmas tree had fallen. He tiptoed out of the bedroom, in case he would waken Josh, and stole down the stairs, or tried to, because every step creaked no matter how quietly he walked. Funny how he never heard those noises during the daytime!

The sitting room door creaked as he opened it. He looked at the Christmas tree and smiled when he saw that it was still standing. It was just as they had left it except that the lights were on. Who could have done that? Mum had put them off when they were going to bed. He was puzzled. Suddenly he felt that someone was watching him. He turned round and it was then he saw him, sitting in the big armchair, with a bag of toys beside him. He was dying to look in the bag but he was afraid Santa would think he had no manners. He tried to say something but couldn't find his voice. He moved a little closer and saw Santa munching the ham sandwich. He looked at Jack with a smile and mustard on his beard.

'Lovely sandwich, Jack.' Jack tried to speak but could only open his mouth and stare at Santa. He stared and stared, rubbed his eyes and finally found his voice.

'Is it really you Santa?'

'It's me, Jack and that sandwich was just lovely. I love ham with a bit of mustard. Only my feet are killing me.' He threw off his big boots and then he spotted Granddad's slippers in the corner.

'Throw me over those slippers. I'll rest my feet for a while.' Jack brought the slippers to him and rubbed his eyes again. Was this all really happening or was he dreaming? He couldn't be sure. He stood looking at Santa who was resting his feet on the hearth.

'Mustn't get too comfortable. I have a lot of houses to visit yet.'

Jack couldn't find the right words. What was he going to do? Granddad needed his slippers to help his sore feet. Sometimes he even wore them during the day. No matter what he did he was going to upset one of them, Granddad or Santa. Even as he tried to think of something to say, he saw Santa putting the slippers into his big bag, so Jack just nodded his head. He couldn't risk annoying Santa. He would deal with Granddad later.

'You'd better get back to bed now,' said Santa, as he pulled on his big boots.

'I must leave toys for you and Josh. I think Josh wants a new bike. I have a splendid one for him, but will you tell him to be careful and not to go flying down the hill. I heard he broke his front teeth on his old bike. Look after him, and promise me you will stay upstairs until morning.'

Jack climbed the stairs not even noticing the squeaking steps. He got into bed quietly, thinking about what had happened. What was he going to do about the slippers? Nobody would believe his story about seeing Santa, least of all Granddad. If his feet got very sore, he might get cranky and that would spoil everybody's

Christmas. Maybe they could all put their money together and buy him a pair in the sales, but that would not be for another week. While he was trying to find a solution, he fell asleep.

Morning came, and Josh was the first to waken.

'Did Santa come?'

'Of course he did,' said Jack. 'He always comes at Christmas. Let's go downstairs and see what he brought.' Down they went together and Jack noticed the stairs didn't creak at all. He must have dreamt it all. Santa had brought lovely toys. Josh got his new bike and some toy cars. Jack got games and books and lots of…

'Anybody seen my slippers?' It was Granddad who was speaking. Jack jumped up.

'Where did you leave them, Granddad?'

'Over there in the corner when I was going to bed.' Jack knew then that he hadn't been dreaming. Or maybe he had!

'I'll look in the kitchen. You often leave them there.' He just wanted to get away until he could think of a way to explain that Santa had sore feet too. After all, Santa deserved the slippers after his hard work. But then Granddad had done loads of work too, putting up the tree, and even tidying the garden. If Granddad couldn't find his slippers, he was likely to get into a really bad mood and would ruin the day for the whole family. Back into the sitting room he went to see Josh pulling out another parcel from under the tree.

'Who is this present for?' he asked.

'It has Granddad's name on it,' said Mum. Granddad looked puzzled as he opened the parcel to see a lovely pair of brand new slippers with a note in one of them which read,

'Thank you for your old slippers, Granddad. Hope you like the new ones. You and I take the same size. Maybe Jack will tell you sometime how I know! Have a nice day and rest your poor feet.' Jack could not believe it! Maybe he would share his secret with Josh tonight when they went to bed. This was going to be the best Christmas ever!

Santa's Little Helper

Once upon a time there was a pretty little girl called Aoife Catherine Mary Gallogly. It was the year 2000 and Christmas was coming. At the North Pole Santa was very busy getting the toys ready for all the boys and girls. Granny had written the letter for Aoife, asking Santa to bring her a 'surprise'. That was fine but guess what? She forgot to tell him where Aoife lived.

Now it was Christmas Eve and Santa was very, very tired. He scratched his head in bewilderment and said, to nobody in particular,

'Where does Aoife live? How am I supposed to know?'

Suddenly a little bird flew down from the big tree behind him.

'I can help, Santa. I can help,' he chirped. 'I know where to find Aoife. She's my friend. I sang to her every morning last summer when her Gran brought her for a walk. When I was leaving she waved to me and said'

"Goodbye little birdie
Fly to the sky
Singing and singing
A merry goodbye".

Santa scratched his head again and the little birdie flapped his wings saying,

'Please let me come, Santa. I can ride on the back of the sleigh if I get tired. It's so very, very far away.'

So Santa and the little bird set off from the North Pole with toys for boys and girls all over the world. The bird had a wonderful time. Each time Santa stopped the birdie perched on Aoife's special parcel, just in case Santa made a mistake and gave her present to someone else. That would never happen. Santa was good at his job but the birdie was taking no chances.

At last they came to Aoife's house. Everything was quiet.

'We're here, Santa. This is where Aoife lives.' While Santa tiptoed around the living room the little bird perched on the window sill of Aoife's bedroom to have a peep. There she was, sound asleep in her cot, dreaming about the surprise that Santa would bring. The little bird was so excited to see her again that he began to chirp, chirp, and chirp. He sang the most beautiful song; he never knew he could sing so well.

Just then Aoife opened her eyes and saw her little friend on the window sill. He was spreading his wings, getting ready to fly away again. Santa still had work to do.

'Goodbye little birdie,' said Aoife. 'You're the nicest surprise anybody could get for Christmas. Will you make sure that Santa goes to all the cousins with toys?'

As she snuggled down into her cot she wondered if her Mama and Dada would believe her next morning or would they think she had been dreaming. She knew she hadn't and she knew too that she was a very special little girl who had a very special little friend. Soon when winter was over her birdie would come again.

Aoife's Visit to the Toyshop

'We'll visit the toyshop tomorrow,' I promised my granddaughter. 'You'll enjoy that'.

The little girl's face lit up with excitement. I had already gone to the new toyshop two weeks before to buy a birthday gift for another little girl. The only thing I remembered about that first hurried visit was that there were plenty of toys from which to choose and it would be a good way to spend a half hour, no more, on what promised to be a wet afternoon. With luck, Aoife would be happy to pick out a toy fairly quickly and then she could come with me while I did my shopping in the supermarket.

As soon as we went into the store, Aoife was delighted with what she saw all around her. She couldn't believe her eyes, row after row of beautiful toys of all makes and shapes, colours and sizes.

'What would you like?' I asked.

'Oh, Granny, I just don't know. Can't we just look at everything?' She was shaking with excitement. How could I refuse! It was almost too much to take in. I resigned myself to spending more than the half hour there. We walked together up and down the aisles, looking at rows and rows of teddies, dolls, toy animals, all waiting for a little boy or girl to choose one of them. Then there were bikes, games and jigsaw puzzles. The toy kitchens were a dream. A big smile told me that this might be what she going to choose. With a bit of luck we could still make the supermarket on time.

'I'll buy this one for your birthday next week,' I said.

'Thank you, Granny. I'd love that. We'll come back again in

a minute after we've looked at the dolls.' I wasn't making much progress as far as the real shopping went.

'Do you like that doll, Aoife?'

'That's not just a doll, Granny. It's a beautiful baby doll.' That was the start of my trip to Wonderland with a little girl who knew how to enjoy a toy store. I was learning! I settled down to listen more carefully to what she had to say.

'I'm just looking at the Barbie clothes. I'm not going to pick them. I want to remember how lovely they look.' This time I said nothing. What was happening to me? I had raced through this store two weeks beforehand, almost annoyed that I couldn't find a doll at once, at the right price of course. Weren't they all, more or less the same? I had seen only what I wanted to see and had never even glanced at all the other toys. Finally, when I had found what I was looking for I had raced to the checkout to pay for the item. A successful trip by my standards. Or was it? This was different. My granddaughter was savouring the joy of a wonderful experience, showing her delight and pleasure with every step. Her enthusiasm was infectious. Suddenly, I began to see it all through the child's eyes, as hand in hand, we looked and talked and walked through the paradise. No! The dolls were not all the same. Some had blue eyes, others brown. Then there were the mammy dolls and the baby ones. There were even those that talked and walked and even drank from a bottle and then proceeded to fill their nappy. The range of clothes was fascinating; ball gowns, evening wear, school wear, rain wear and all kinds of wear. Aoife explained it all to me. Her imagination was a revelation. She had a story to tell with every step we took.

'That little puppy is lonely. We must find his mammy. Look on top, Granny. Can you find her?' And I did. I was seeing it all in a different light now. This was a new awakening, no longer something to be endured but a sharing of simple joys and pleasures. We were in a world of magic and time was no longer important.

Aoife did choose the toy kitchen and the baby doll and finally we left the store hand in hand. We had shared something special and wonderful and I was just as happy as she was. When I finally looked at my watch I realised that we had been in the store for over two hours. The shopping could wait. I could do it anytime. My granddaughter would only be with me for a few days and there were more important things to do than household shopping. How could kitchen rolls and beans and toilet rolls compete with what we had seen? We had spent a wonderful time together. I will never go into that store again without remembering those shining eyes and that happy little face. It's true when they say it's all about attitude. It depends on how we see it!